Red the *Rooster* and Rocko the Mean *Butterfly* in Stories from the Barnyard

Red the *Rooster* and Rocko the Mean *Butterfly* in Stories from the Barnyard

JOHN E. DEMPSEY

ARCHWAY PUBLISHING

Archway Publishing books may be ordered through booksellers or by contacting:

Archway Publishing
1663 Liberty Drive
Bloomington, IN 47403
www.archwaypublishing.com
1 (888) 242-5904

ISBN: 978-1-4808-3649-5 (sc)
ISBN: 978-1-4808-3650-1 (e)

Library of Congress Control Number: 2016914469

Print information available on the last page.

Archway Publishing rev. date: 10/06/2016

Contents

Dedication:

I would like to dedicate this book to my wife Zhi
and daughters Sarah and Shannon who were indispensible
in every phase of it's development.

Introduction

This book had a somewhat accidental beginning. On a cold February day, I was looking out the window into the snow-covered world and realizing I was now an empty-nester. My two daughters had grown up, and one now lived in San Francisco after graduating from Hamilton College. The other was at the University of Rochester. I really missed the pitter-patter of kids in the house. It was just my wife and me now.

I decided to make an effort to stay connected, and I decided to write a letter to them each week. The first letter was full of memories and compliments and boiled down to me saying that I missed them very much. I realized then and there that I had to come up with a better vehicle. I remembered how I used to tell them stories about Red and Rocko when they were tiny kids.

Red was a rooster in the barnyard who was very good at solving problems, and Rocko was a butterfly who had a bad disposition but also almost magical powers to understand and solve problems. It was a gentle transition to realize that I could make up stories about Red and Rocko and send them off to Sarah and Shannon.

So in February 2015, I began to send off a story a week of the exploits of Red and Rocko. This was all under the guise of communicating now with my adult children. It was fun, and it worked mostly because I usually wrote them a short personal note on the back of the Red and Rocko stories.

Now I want to qualify these children's stories. They have all the trappings of stories for children, but they have some very uncharacteristic qualities for this genre. For example, there are vocabulary words that usually would not show up in books for this age group. This comes from when the girls were young. I used to put a difficult vocabulary word up on the refrigerator, and the girls would have to define it during dinnertime. This process was now transferred into these children's stories. A lot of them are buried there, and for any young reader, it should trigger the need to keep a dictionary handy while reading the adventures in the barnyard.

Another mismatch with the children's genre is that I describe and use incidents and plots that are definitely not suited for young people's consumption. This goes back to another family tradition where I always told the girls the truth about the world around them. It was usually done in terms of black Irish humor. There was more to this, however. It was about really describing the world around us in some very honest and simple terms. Because of this, these stories might better be picked through by an adult before being read to very small children.

Another incongruity is that stories like "A Love Song" or "A Simple Birdsong" are not really children's stories at all but rather a dive into a worldview description. You might ask why I put them into a children's story. But I contend that children are actually hungry for a peek over the fence into the grown-up world.

These stories accomplish this gently and hopefully without any dogmatic insults to the young reader's consciousness. The overarching attempt here is to be whimsical and playful while keeping some connections to what we unfortunately call reality. I hope, by keeping these politically incorrect qualities in this book, I have, on the flip side, respected the imagination, genius, and natural intelligence of the young reader.

I hope the reader—either young or old—finds entertainment and meaning in these simple short stories. In addition the invisible benefit and ultimate accomplishment would be that these stories provide a platform and starting point from which the young reader begins to exercise his or her own imagination.

The Fox Learns His Lesson

J ust a quick note: I, as usual, don't have much that you are not already aware of, but that's the nature of modern communications. So I am left here to communicate the more mundane stuff. So at any rate, I thought I'd tell you a story about this butterfly, Rocko. Oh, maybe you've heard of him. He goes by the name of Rocko the Mean Butterfly.

It all started down at the henhouse, and you know who ruled the roost there, Red the Rooster. He was having trouble with this fox, who kept coming around and trying to catch one of the hens alone so he could have a nice snack. So far he had not managed to complete his fowl plan, but he was persistent, and Red knew it was only a matter of time before one of his hens would relax and be caught off guard. At first he didn't know what to do. He was plenty mad about that fox, but he was, after all, a chicken. He actually considered calling 9-1-1, but the last time he did that, they made fun of him. And when they showed up, they were very late and of no use to Red anyway.

Then it hit him. He said, "I'll call Rocko the Mean Butterfly. He will know what to do."

So he waited out in the hen yard the following afternoon to see if he would run into Rocko. Rocko often would come and hang around the flowers on the side of the chicken coop, and Red had many pleasant afternoon swapping stories with Rocko about their many adventures.

But today was different. Red was just a bit anxious and nervous because he never knew when that fox might up the ante and become braver. His dear flock of hens were at stake here, and Red, for all his toughness, really did have some deep and wonderful feelings for his hens.

Later in the afternoon, when the wind had died down and the smell of the flowers lingered in the animal yard, there he was, flitting from flower to flower, doing what butterflies do best. If anyone could just see him there among the flowers, they would never believe the amazing adventures this butterfly could tell.

Red wasted no time when he saw Rocko. He strode over and clucked a greeting. Rocko returned the greeting but had found a particularly good bunch of flowers and did not want to be disturbed at this particular time. He continued his mystical dance with the flowers, lost in the wonderful nectar and hypnotic effect of pollen.

Red was annoyed and persisted, clucking and doing things roosters do in dramatic fashion. Anyway, not to belabor the point, this clucking and wing flapping, not to mention the dramatic ground scratching, did get Rocko's attention. Now for all his meanness and reputation to that effect, Rocko was also somewhat of a good citizen. He stopped, turned, and not only acknowledged Red but gave him his full attention.

Red explained the situation to Rocko and admitted he was not only concerned but worried that one of these days one of his wonderful hens might end up as a meal for the fox. Rocko was never one to jump to conclusions and liked to think things over, as you can remember from previous stories about him. Red continued to explain how the fox would slink about at dusk, and while he and his hens were very proud to be free-range chickens, this did increase the danger from the fox since, in the barnyard, there were hundreds of places to hide. A blitzkrieg attack by the fox could happen at any time and would be over in an instance. Red went on to explain how the sadness and grieving from an event like this, however, would continue for days, if not weeks.

Rocko was not listening though. He had begun to imagine a defensive and indeed an offensive response to this most wily of all predators. Red wanted to know what the strategy was. Rocko put him off, saying he would do his best to keep his hens safe and to never mind because he himself was not absolutely sure of the outcome but reassured Red he was working on it.

Later that evening Red took confidence from the fact that he saw Rocko flitting in the trees above the barnyard. That confidence turned to muscle-jumping anxiety and persistent fear when he saw a shadow move upon another shadow in the shadowed part of the barnyard. Most of the other animals had eaten and were taking their after-dinner siesta. It was quiet but with a strong tension in the air of the barnyard. Dread and worry filled Red as he realized that Mable and Georgia were walking about gossiping with not a concern in the world.

Red, sitting on his perch next to the chicken coop door, where he usually could survey the entire barnyard, gulped a deep-throated concern when he saw Mable and Georgia come around the large oak at the same time as the shadow, swift on quiet footfalls, turned into the fox with mouth agape and headed in full flight toward his two distracted and totally unconcerned lovers.

Rocko had seen it even before Red and was already hovering above the ground between the fox and his intended meal. Now a lot of people don't realize it, but butterflies usually start typhoons, cyclones, and sometimes hurricanes. It's a little known fact of the natural world that, by flapping their wings in a certain particular fashion, the butterflies can stir up a vortex of swirling wind that, once started, takes on a life of its own. Now if just for a moment we can freeze this potentially terrifying scenario taking place in the courtyard while the scientific phenomenon of butterfly tornadoes can be examined just a bit closer.

Rocko was creating a medium vortex of whirling wind, not too much so it would alert the fox, but enough so that, as he passed through it, the fox would be lifted off the ground and placed where Rocko's butterfly wings directed the now-screaming vortex of violent wind. It was always a challenge to avoid the spinoffs from that much wind for a butterfly, but Rocko knew just how to not only avoid his masterful creation but also to send it in a direction of his choice. So in this particular opportunity, he flapped and stopped and flapped and moved his wings in a delicate dance learned a thousand years ago by ancient butterflies. The effect was that he directed the tornado down away from the farm into a rather large briar patch so all the branches would break up the tornado and drop its holdings into the middle of that there briar patch.

Rocko watched with satisfaction as the tornado hit the briar patch, and the gnarled intertwining vines of the briar patch interrupted the swirling wind. There out of the top of the tornado, like a football kicked for a field goal, the fox came hurling down toward those nasty thorn-laden bushes. He smiled as he heard the ohhhhs, ahhhhs, and screams of sheer pain from the fox. He flew over to Red and told him that he did not think the fox would present any serious problems for quite some time.

Red thanked Rocko profusely but seemed in such a hurry. As Rocko was flying away, he saw Red scolding Mable and Georgia. He was gesturing, squawking, and doing all things a rooster has to do to love and protect a clutch of hens.

Rocko just shook his head in bewilderment. Butterfly love was so much easier.

Listening to Nature

I went over to the barnyard to see if there was anything there worthy of reporting. It's usually pretty boring, but there always seems to be something going on over there. Sad to say, nothing was happening in the barnyard as I wandered around and greeted the animals.

The day was warm, so I decided to walk across the meadow behind the barn. Out of sheer boredom, I ended up walking all the way down to the creek where the willow trees are. I guess I was drawn to that place because folks have used it as a picnic spot in the past. I was staying in the shade of the willows and congratulating myself on accepting the banality of the day when I realized I was not alone.

Perched on one of the lower limbs of a willow tree sat Rocko. He had seen me coming, and once I entered voice distance, he greeted me politely. I returned the greeting and added in haste that I hoped I was not invading his solitary meditation.

He said, "No, I was just sitting and enjoying the moment."

I relaxed a bit because I had disturbed Rocko on previous occasions and felt frightened when he became, shall we say, less than friendly.

Making an attempt at conversation, I asked, "Do you spend a lot of time alone?"

Rocko looked at me and smiled. "Butterflies are never alone unless they are very high up in the air."

"How's that?" I didn't understand either the smile or the comment.

"Well, while it's true that we are animals, we have strong relationships with many plants and commune with them on a daily basis." He then nodded toward a number of plants nearby. "These are all my friends."

My cupboard of curiosity had been opened. "How do you communicate with them?"

"Your senses are all separate," said Rocko, "while a butterfly's senses are all combined. We can pick up vibrations from most plants. What we can't hear or see, we can always smell or just feel. The truth is, while a lot of the interchange is not objective, it does communicate unbelievable beauty and delicate emotions that don't exist in the animal world. The vitality of communication among plants is much richer than animal communication."

I felt like an explorer on a new planet. Maybe it was just too much information to take in all at once.

Rocko saw my dismay and confusion. "It's just part of naturally being a butterfly. I didn't mean to confuse you."

"No," I said, "It's just hard to understand from my position."

"Well, let me try a little experiment," said Rocko. "I had this butterfly friend who used to go after the pollen from places like the University of Rochester and Hamilton College, and he taught me a trick."

Rocko instructed me to go about fifteen feet in front of him and sit at the base of a willow tree. He then explained that he was going to flail his wings in a very special way to force my senses together. He explained that this would give a rough version of what a butterfly feels from all his surrounding friends. I wouldn't be able to communicate back the way butterflies can, but for a short time, I would listen in on the plant world.

Sitting there, I tried to clear my mind as Rocko instructed me to close my eyes. At first there was nothing. Slowly I began to sense that I could hear the smell of the willows and feel all the plants around me, eager to communicate with a new creature. I opened my eyes and could hear the blue sky and see the wind. It was like everything doubled down on itself, emphatically announcing its existence and living presence.

My one sense, now a collection of all my senses, gathered it all in and wanted more. This small, quiet place among the willows became a picnic and party where all sorts of energies entered and competed for attention. At first it was sort of overwhelming, but as I retreated into myself in self-defense, I realized that a lot of the communication going on was among and between other plants and not directed at me at all.

As I quieted down, I realized the willow tree I was leaning against had been singing to me. Its song was sad, old, and hopeful and was somehow modulated by the wind as it blew through its branches. I have to say that the very ancient quality of this song carried a buoyant, hopeful promise. As I listened, I could hear the earthworms tickle the roots of the willow tree. It all went into the song. In this song without words, the tree told me it was happy and glad to be able to share with me.

I reluctantly tore my attention away from the singing willow because a growing cadence of a moan was coming from the grasses surrounding me. This moan was similar to the chant of some Tibetan monks. Its resonance spoke to the inside of me. Billions of life-forms were saying hello in this deep vibration of life. While the willow had been different, the grasses were something familiar and friendly. I was inside their chant, and it carried me effortlessly to an understanding that grasses give life to many other life-forms. My chest was not big enough to carry the pleasure of this chant and the information it carried.

The wildflowers spread among the willows down by the creek here were crying for attention. This strange escape from pleasure allowed me to shift my attention into the delicate, exquisite, elegant pandemonium of the music of the wildflowers. They gave because it was their nature to give. That was immediately obvious in their communication. There was an unsettling freedom communicated in their sound that is hard to describe. It was sometimes shrill, occasionally soft, and at times totally seductive.

In one heartbeat, I was back sitting against the willow with all my senses separate and working. I immediately felt like crying.

Rocko looked at me and smiled. "It's enough that you should know that this other world exists. Don't tell anyone what I did for you today. Certain powers would be upset to know that this world was shared with you."

I was still in a state of wonder at what I had experienced. In truth, I'm still in a state of wonder at what happened even though it's been a few days now since I promised Rocko I wouldn't tell anyone. The thing is that some things are so wonderful that it's just impossible to keep them locked up inside of you. That's why I'm telling you, but please don't tell anyone, okay?

Thelma

I know there is a definite line between gossip and news. I thought this story fell closer to the gossip line, but it did have parts to it regarding news of the barnyard so I felt negligent if I did not report on it. Simply, Thelma the Cow thinks there are ghosts in the barn. She won't go into the barn alone, and her milk has really fallen off. Everyone else has tried to reassure her, but for several reasons that I will describe, Thelma is convinced the barn has visitors from the other side.

This didn't become apparent until a few weeks ago when she got all psychotic about going into the barn alone in the middle of the day. This particular episode was worsened by the fact that a couple goats were present there when this happened, and they are about as sensitive as a pitchfork on hay. They started to laugh at Thelma and, in their grand fashion, made up what they thought was a very creative poem about the situation, "Thelma Welma Is a Scarity Cow."

They repeated this ad nauseam, which you can well imagine didn't help matters at all. It wasn't bad enough that Thelma was insulted then by the goats, but they thought themselves so creative in this ditty that they repeated it every time they saw Thelma out and about.

A number of other animals that had stalls next to Thelma tried to reassure and console her. It didn't seem to have much effect, and Thelma continued to agonize over the fact that some type of spirits or spooks were inhabiting the barn. She described hearing noises and seeing shadows, She said that, being alone did not frightened her, except that late at night, she heard a scary voice calling her name.

Mildred the Mare tried to explain that away, "The barn has wind blowing through it, and sometimes it sounds like someone whispering at night."

Thelma rebutted Mildred, "The voice I heard said bad things and suggested hideous and repulsive things could happen to me."

She had even tried to shout back at this voice, but that just reinforced its macabre and morbid suggestions. The other animals did not share Thelma's fears but did recognize that her apprehension and dread were very real. Several spoke to the terror and panic these apparitions had caused in Thelma. They doubted the cause but saw that the effect was very real.

It really got to be a serious problem because it came to the point where Thelma was scared to go into the barn alone and would wait for the other animals before she ventured into her stall area. She was nervous and always on edge. The other cows and horses consulted among themselves and came up with an idea. Bossie the Cow promised to stay close to Thelma throughout the night. This did seem to quiet her somewhat, and everyone held their breath as night approached and the animals returned to their quarters. Everything went quite peacefully until Bossie fell asleep.

Thelma woke her in a fit of anxiety, "The voices said they are sending rats to get my milk."

It took Bossie the rest of the night to quiet Thelma down. The other animals questioned Bossie in the morning.

She honestly reported, "I heard no voices."

But she did admit to dozing off. A seed planted takes a while to sprout. The other animals looked into each other's faces to see if there was anything credible there. The phantom makes his mark by leaving none. The community's imagination began to fill in the invisible blanks. Mildred the mare became concerned and decided to tell Red the rooster about this. She wanted to see if he didn't have any suggestions about what to do.

Red acknowledged that he had heard of Thelma's plight and was already quite sick of hearing, "Thelma Welma is a scarity cow."

Red went up to the barn and talked to Thelma. In truth, he mostly just listened because at this point, Thelma was telling everyone about the noises and scary voices. Red was quiet after he listened to Thelma, and after a bit, he said he would consult with Rocko the Mean Butterfly.

Rocko showed up the very next day and asked to see Thelma. He said it was all very intriguing, but he would like to spend some time with Thelma, both day and night. This was very interesting, and everyone was really quite curious as to the effect this would have. Most of the first day, Rocko, like Red, just listened, but Rocko heard the story of how Thelma had lost a calf the year before and had quite a difficult time afterward.

The evening approached, and Rocko had quieted Thelma down to the point where she could go into the barn with only minor anxiety. They settled in for the night with Rocko stationed on the stall wall just above and near to Thelma's good ear. (She had poor hearing in her right ear.) On cue, the noises came accompanied by the changing shadows, and Rocko's reassurance kept Thelma quietly attentive.

The rest of the barn slipped into sleep, and it was then that Thelma reported to Rocko that she was hearing the voices. Rocko's counsel to Thelma in that critical moment was to remain absolutely quiet and listen.

"Remember," whispered Rocko, "silence is the way God prays."

They listened and remained completely silent. The voices became weaker and evaporated back into the nightly sounds of the barn. Thelma turned to Rocko and smiled. You have to hang around cows for a bit to recognize a smile. It was there, and along with it came a tremendous relief in Thelma.

She thanked Rocko but asked if he wouldn't stay for the rest of the night just so she could get used to this new reality and not be inadvertently tricked by some sound back into her now-vanishing fear. Rocko reassured her that he would be right there next to her as long as she needed his help.

Now the interesting thing about all this was that Thelma's episode of frailty and fear had, as I previously mentioned, seeded an idea in the community. Ideas like ghosts, goblins, and voices in the night have a way of taking on a reality of their own. The other animals in the barnyard had by this time absorbed enough of this to really begin to scare and sensitize themselves.

It was interesting because each new sound or shadow now had multiple causes. Everyone was just a bit on edge as night crept into the barnyard. It took longer to fall asleep, and once they did, it was a restless sleep, and the minor noises of the mice in the night became possible monsters.

The next day after one of the first good night of sleep in a long time, Thelma was walking down to the pasture. She passed the goat pen and heard the old refrain, "Thelma Welma is a scarity cow."

Thelma waited just a moment while the goats all sniggered to themselves over their creative poem. She turned and said in her loud cow voice, "Boo!" The goats all jumped and began to run into each other. Thelma walked away with a cow smile, thinking to herself, *It's great to make some real progress.*

A New Use for Rabbits

I was wandering around somewhat aimlessly in the barnyard as it got on toward evening the other day and happened by the rabbit hutch when I heard Josephine the mother rabbit telling her kittens that, if they behaved, she would tell them a bedtime story. Now I'm always interested in experiencing different aspects of the barnyard culture, and this seemed like a wonderful opportunity to listen in on a different world.

I peeked in on the hutch and saw about seven or eight small bunnies all snuggled up in a corner together. They appeared warm, comfortable, and ready for a bedtime story. Josephine was busy at the other end of the hutch, but I could see that she was getting ready to come over and parent her small ones to sleep. The little ones jostled gently against each other in anticipation of the promised bedtime story.

Josephine came over and settled in right in front of her batch of youngsters. She told these bunnies a rather strange story, which I will try to tell again to you here for what it's worth.

"In the forest quite nearby here," said Josephine, "lives an ogre. This ogre has a terrible disposition and doesn't much like anyone. He stays to himself and pointedly avoids all unnecessary contact with other living things."

Josephine continued her story and kept her small ones hypnotized by the tone and content of her narrative. "Sometimes, as is always the case, songbirds come and sing outside the window. If this happens to the ogre, he yells and curses so loud that, first of all, you can't even hear the songbirds, but second, the birds themselves can't stand the discordant sounds that the ogre makes.

"It's been said that his growl is so nasty that it can curdle milk. All of the smaller animals always avoid where the ogre lives, and they also studiously avoid any places where they know or suspect he will go. Larger animals like the deer, elk, and bear also avoid any contact with the ogre because they've learned from past experience that he will confront them and pick a fight. He delights in fighting, and the bigger the adversary, the more he likes it. He's never been known to lose a fight, and he often brags about that fact to see if he can't entice a doubtful adversary into conflict. A lot of the time, when no one will step up and enter into open conflict with him, he will wait at different places where he knows certain animals will pass and then confront and humiliate them just for fun.

"Why, I remember one time when Norma the Deer was minding her own business, grazing in the pasture. And the ogre came upon her and told her that the pasture she was grazing in was all reserved for just him. Now Norma knew that was not true, but she did not want to argue with an obvious bully, so she tried to leave the pasture. He stopped her, saying he wanted the grass back that she had already eaten. He taunted and threatened her in such a persistent way that eventually Norma threw up all the grass she had just previously eaten.

"There was also the case of the beavers who had built their dam and lodge in the creek and were just doing what beavers do when the ogre decided he didn't want them there. He waded into the stream and broke their dam every day for two months. And in addition to that, he would jump up and down on their lodge until it caved in. Beavers, as everyone knows, are very industrious, but his persistence in harassment was so continuous that even they eventually gave in and moved.

"There was also the case of the foxes who thought themselves very clever and would run through his territory in a stealthy way when they thought he wasn't looking. He surprised them one day by catching two of them and then tying their tails together and watching them fight until they were exhausted and near death.

"There was also the story told round the creek about the woodchuck who had his den off and away from the ogre's turf. The ogre decided he didn't want the woodchuck to have his den there anymore and told the woodchuck to move. The woodchuck just would go down underground into his den whenever he suspected the ogre was near. He thought, as long as he did that, there was not much that the ogre could do, so he felt rather safe. The ogre surprised him by digging along his burrow and making it big enough for the ogre to pass. He dug right down to the lower den and grabbed the woodchuck while he was asleep." Josephine refrained from finishing the story about what happened to the poor woodchuck.

"Now this misanthrope had widened his field of hate to all creatures. He just didn't like anyone. He proved this, each and every day, by finding ways to be nasty to all the other living creatures he met. Now there is one strange bump in this complete landscape of hate. Whenever the ogre comes upon rabbits, he isn't mean to them, but he's very meticulous about capturing them. He puts them in a cage, feeds them, and keeps them safe."

Now the baby rabbits had been paying attention and were, to say the least, baffled by this strange twist in an otherwise predictable fairy tale. It moved them to shift a bit in their now warm and comfortable sleeping spot.

"Why does the ogre who is mean to everyone treat the rabbits differently?" asked one of Josephine's little ones.

"Well, that is why I'm telling you this important story," said Josephine. "I want to make sure you never go down and across the creek to where they say the ogre lives."

"We won't! We won't!" spouted a chorus of small voices. "But why does the ogre capture bunny rabbits?" they asked in unison.

"Well," said Josephine, "I want to be honest with you and tell you the truth. The ogre uses little, tiny bunny rabbits for toilet paper because they are soft and furry. This horrible truth is compounded by the fact that we think the ogre has IBS."

"What's IBS?" asked a now-horrified group of small rabbits.

"It's irritable bowel syndrome," said Josephine.

Now I'm not sure who was more traumatized by this fairy tale, the small bunnies or me. I looked into the hutch and saw a truly terrified group of small bunnies. Now I know that this is supposed to be a children's story and this bit of information about the ogre somewhat crosses the line about what's proper and appropriate to tell small children.

I think Josephine was trying to educate her small ones in the ways of the world, so I guess telling them where the hazards are was fair game. I, however, could not help thinking about those poor, little bunny rabbits.

A Tale 5 of Tails

The barnyard is always a hotbed of political and social narrative so I thought it interesting to find what the animals had turned their attention to. All the animals were bragging or describing the merits of their tails. I don't know how this all got started, but when I walked through the barnyard, all the conversation was about tails. It was somewhat interesting because it was one area where I was out of the loop as it were. In this environment, I was critiqued for my lack of this important appendage.

I had just finished listening to Mildred the Mare describing how the horse's tail is the best and most perfect example of this extremity. Some of the pigs who had been listening to Mildred turned their attention on me and noted, not only do we feeding hands not have a tail, the lack of that extremity was the cause of us beginning to unnaturally walk on just two feet. They went on to describe how that behavior defeated the biology of our bodies and did a great disservice to our species.

There was general agreement among the animals present that the feeding hands lost something important once we lost our tails. Feeling a bit defensive against the agreement in the crowd, I pointed out, "Perhaps it's better to have no tail than one that looks like a curly fry and seems to not be useful at all."

All the pigs present blushed red at the insult and stumbled against one another to rebut my claim. George reclaimed the attention of the group and stated with some merit that the pigs' tails were not only elegant in their simplicity but whimsical in their presentation. There was a type of passive agreement about the pigs' tails, but even then I could see that they were not going to win the Tail of the Year Award.

The goats were all in a hurry to describe the beauty and uniqueness of their tails. They pointed out, unlike other animals, the goat tail was just the right length with just the right amount of fur and decoration on it.

This brought a quizzical look from some of the other animals.

Goner the Goose, who was always picking fights he couldn't possibly win, said with some disdain, "It appears to me that goat tails are the messiest of all places in the barnyard." This was just a polite way of saying they always had a bit of poop on them.

Everyone was impressed with Goner's diplomacy. It ultimately didn't matter because the insult went right over the goats' heads.

The cows wanted to place their tails in contention for the most efficient and perfectly designed ones in the barnyard. Everyone always listened with some degree of respect to the cows' pronouncements. They had a position in the community that warranted that. That deferment did not, however, include anyone actually agreeing with them, especially on such a pertinent issue as to whose tail was the best. The criticism of the cows' comments were scathing, critical, and, I think, accurate.

One of the swans said it best to Thelma the cow, "Just because it's attached to you doesn't make it beautiful." I actually thought that was a curious statement for a swan to make. Red the Rooster had been on the sidelines, listening to this debate and wanting to make some comments. Everyone fell silent because they wanted to hear what Red would say about this important topic.

He said, "Everyone's tails were beautiful in their own way and appeared to serve their owners with some degree or purpose. Saying that, however, does not rule out the reality that, if you don't have feathers in your tails, you're really not in contention for the beautiful tail awards."

This immediately brought cheers from the geese, ducks, swans, and goats. Someone had to explain to the goats that they did not have feathers in their tails, so they felt a bit sheepish about cheering that last announcement.

Red's statement caused a degree of consternation among the larger animals, and at first it went unchallenged. Mildred the Mare, however, ventured a comment to the effect that she was not even sure that plumage like that could be categorized as a tail. This poignant and intuitive comment inserted a passion back into the argument, and everyone wanted to talk at once. Red was amazed that the equity of his authority as a barnyard leader did not translate into describing who had the best tail.

The geese rushed into the argument, "Of all the feathered backsides, ours are the most useful and beautiful."

Now the one thing geese are good at is getting conformity in the ranks, and as this announcement was made, a chorus of agreement went up from the ranks of the geese that made it sound like there was overwhelming support for that position. The swans, however, were watching and listening, and although they were not half their number, the swans dampened the geese cheering section by stating, "Saying something loudly does not make it true."

I could see that the swans wanted to present their case for having the most beautiful and elegant tail feathers, but the ducks beat them to the starting gate. The ducks stumbled over themselves describing their efficient and most useful of all tail feathers.

They said, "Our tail feathers work both in air and water, and unlike some fowl present here, our tail feathers are not overdone."

The swans were very dismissive of the other feathered animals and started to describe their process of synchronous molting, which started to put everyone present to sleep. What the swans thought as a high-level description of swan tail feathers disintegrated into a session where they were ridiculed and jeered. I could just tell that everyone thought the swans felt like they were legends in their own minds.

I saw from the various descriptions about tails that we feeding hands had truly lost something important once we lost our tails. They are useful to express emotion, to communicate, and especially to say good-bye. I wondered at that for just a moment and speculated what courtship would have been like if we had tails. Would curling your tail with someone mean something quite intimate and lead to greater things? These and associated thoughts haunted me after this go-round with tails.

I walked around the barnyard, and everyone was quite adamant to convince the other that their tail was superior in some way. It was interesting listening to the conviction and passion the various animals had about their tails. This topic remained high on everyone's agenda for quite a number of days, but eventually they just seemed to leave it behind them.

I continued to muse over this issue, however. The possibilities were endless. Would we as males have a way with our tails that added swagger to our walk? Would it be a useful addendum when meeting someone new? Would there be situations where the tail became quiet and communicated an attempt at being humble? Oh, who could we be if only we had tales?

Unhinged

I t's somewhat weird that something dangerous and potentially hurtful can also be funny. An event happened in the barnyard this past week that qualified to be put into that category. Now I don't want to appear sadistic or mean so I'll try to the best of my ability to just describe to you what happened without any editorial comment. You can either see the humor for yourself or not.

First let me describe the instigating cause and the resulting pandemonium it caused. On the west side of the barn is a rather large door for the horses to enter and leave the barn without opening the larger doors on the end of the barn. This door is quite large and on some very well-oiled hinges. On many days, this door is left open, and many of the animals use it for ingress and leaving the building.

Usually because the door swings quite freely, the door is propped open by way of a hook that is attached to the side of the building. Now for some reason that no one apparently knows, this hook was not connected or became unlatched at some point on this day. This on any given normal day would not have presented a problem. It just so happened on this particular day that a strong breeze came up from the meadow and blew against the barn. This vagrant stop-and-go wind had the effect of blowing this door open and shut alternatively, depending on the whimsy of the wind god.

This also would not have caused any problems except for the timing of Disney's exit from the barn. Disney was not this goat's real name, but everyone called him that because he somewhat lived in a pretend world. His real name was Walt. When Disney was leaving the barn, a good gust of wind came up and blew the door shut. The door slammed shut, hitting Disney quite hard and knocking him a good one. The door was quite heavy, and the gust of wind was strong, so Disney took a pretty good hit.

Disney got up after being slammed and wanted to fight whoever had walloped him. A nearby pig who had witnessed the whole thing explained to Disney what had happened. This is where this story sort of takes on a humorous note because, at that point with the explanation given, Disney wanted to retaliate against the door.

"No, no, no," said the pig. "It was not an intentional act. It was a combination of the door not being latched and the wind coming up at just the right moment."

A number of the other barnyard animals had begun to gather because they sensed an event in the making. It doesn't take much to create a crowd in the barnyard. The pig could see that his explanation confused the goat, who wanted someone to blame for the hit he had taken.

Disney turned to the pig and asked in a rather angry tone, "But why did the door swing closed so hard then?"

The pig, who was honestly trying to explain this natural event in logical terms, turned to the goat. "Well, you see the door is on some well-oiled hinges, and that allows it to swing freely even if it's just the wind as the motivating force."

The goat now focused on the hinges of this rather large door, and if looks could kill, those hinges would have been in real trouble. Now you have to understand something about goats. They're not really bright. There is more going on between two sticks rubbed together than when a goat is thinking hard. They just aren't really good at figuring certain things out. On top of that, once they get an idea in their head, they are like a stick in the creek. They just go with the flow. Disney was a perfect example of the lower end of this spectrum.

Disney let loose a long course of mundane curses at these hinges. He repeated a lot of the same vitriolic words because his vocabulary was limited, but he wanted to show his great displeasure at the causative agent in his mishap. His monologue was directed at these hinges as if they could understand what he was saying. Now a number of the animals who had taken the role of audience in this scenario now began to see the humor in this situation.

The timing of their laughter was gasoline to Disney's anger. Now my mother always told me not to laugh at anyone who doesn't know any better. This would have been good advice for this particular situation. Unfortunately my mother and no other mothers were in sight at that moment. The laughter cut to the quick. Disney was hurt twice now. It took a moment, but all of that translated into blind, massive, flaming anger.

Disney put down his head and charged the door in a rage. The door was half open, so when he hit it with his head, it swung back against the barn and bounced off it, rebounding out again against Disney. To Disney, this was challenge accepted. Don Quixote tilted at windmills, and now Disney was in a fight to the death with a door. The number of animals congregating to witness the contest of wills between the goat and the door was growing.

Now in the comfort of your chair reading this, there is no danger, tension, or challenge involved. This was not the case with poor Disney. This unfortunate, miserable goat believed he was in the fight of his life. He had hit the door, and it had reciprocated in kind.

Disney put his head down again and charged. In the intervening seconds, the door had drifted back against the barn, so when Disney hit it this time, there was absolutely no give. Goats are good head-butters, but the barn door back against the barn was an immovable object.

Disney staggered back a few steps and knew in that moment he had been bested.. Now in truth, we are all the same. Frustrated in our efforts, we retreat to a very empty place inside of ourselves. This is where Disney went. He let out a goat moan that lamented the birth of the earth itself. The sadness and sorrow of this deplorable wail caught all the bystanders off guard.

A moment ago, they were watching a funny episode with a goat. Now hearing the grief-stricken voice of defeat, they were cheering for a goat against a door. We are all part of the herd. We recognize defeat and want to protest even if it's back again tilting at windmills.

Red the Rooster happened by just as this had taken place. He listened with curiosity as the bystanders sympathized with Disney and denigrated the doors hinges. He said, "You know the Irish have a saying. 'I hope the hinges of our relationship never get rusty.'"

He walked away giggling. The crowd, the goat, and the door sorted things out soon after that, but it was a story that went round the barnyard for days thereafter.

The Shirt That Was a Goat

I know I usually report on conditions or events in the barnyard, but a strange thing happened to me that I should bring to your attention. Now before I tell you what happened, I just want to disclose my misgivings about telling you about this. It's just that I don't want this story to impact your value for the previous reporting about the barnyard. Let me proceed, and you will see why I have some caution about telling you about this event.

I came home after a hard day's work, and I was dusty and dirty so I was changing to take a shower. I took off my shirt and threw it on the floor, and I was about to go to the shower when I noticed that my shirt had fallen into a form that looked like a young goat. It was uncanny because, as I looked at this form made from a dirty shirt, it had all the earmarks of a goat. At first I laughed at this lifeless form but then absentmindedly said to it, "Why aren't you just the spitting image of some of my barnyard friends?"

And this is the strange part. It replied back, "Yes, it appears I've taken the form of a goat for you."

Now at this juncture, I must admit that the voice of the goat somewhat came from within my own mind. I recognized this and sensed I was playing tricks upon myself. Now I additionally immediately knew this was not real because the "shirt" was not speaking goat. So in that sense, I was not worried at this point at all. In fact I actually chided the shirt by saying, "Well, now aren't you a cheeky bastard?"

At this point, the goat/shirt said, "This is a children's story, and you shouldn't curse."

I laughed out loud. "What are you talking about? You're a shirt, a stupid, lifeless, dirty shirt lying on the floor pretending to talk to me."

"Now wait a minute," said the goat. "I grant you the curious circumstance, but if indeed I'm just an illusion in your mind, am I not worth listening to?"

"I don't know," I said. "It's a bit sketchy because then it's like I'm talking to myself with an excuse involved."

"The excuse," said the goat/shirt, "is that I'm a shirt that looks like a goat."

At this point I circled the goat/shirt and looked at it from every angle. I must admit I was a bit upset with myself for indulging this goat/shirt even a little bit. I took my foot and disarranged the shirt so the goat disappeared.

Pleased with myself for regaining control of my world, I proceeded to take my shower. While in the shower, I stated to laugh at myself for even rearranging the shirt to get rid of the goat. Was that really necessary?

I got out of the shower, dried myself, and threw the towel onto the tile floor. And damn it! There was that goat again. I was somewhat ready this time, however. I thought of the poet Shelley who said, "Reason respects the differences, and imagination the similitudes of things"

"Why is it you have come to visit me?" I asked the goat with sarcasm.

"Oh, just to talk," said the goat with an equally caustic quality to his voice.

"Am I chiding myself with an attitude in your voice?" I said.

"Whatever do you mean?" said the towel/goat.

"Look," I said, "I know I'm just really talking to myself."

"Wait," said the towel/goat. "The ghosts in the branches of the trees at night in a windstorm are real. Not real in the sense that you will ever capture them and lock them up. But real in the sense that they fill your mind with images and ideas that move you physically, emotionally, and spiritually."

"Oh God!" I said. "A towel is lecturing me!"

"Okay," said the towel/goat, "I'm going to tell you a secret."

"Oh, gee! This ought to be good," I said. "Did I forget to dry my butt after the shower?"

"Well, see," said the towel/goat. "That's just the wrong attitude to receive what I have to give."

Now I have to admit here that, at that point in the conversation, I did have somewhat of an epiphany. It was just this. If the towel that looked like a goat that was talking to me was really just my mind disguising itself so it could better communicate with me, the conscious self, I was/am somewhat crazy. However,

I thought I'd just received the information that there was a secret involved, and in truth I love secrets.

"Okay," I said to the towel/goat. "I'm all ears for the secret."

The towel/goat laughed and said with a weird authority that I had approached him the wrong way. In all honesty, the towel/goat didn't really laugh as much as I heard him chortle. I guess what I'm saying is that a note was dropped in the symphony I was listening to. The illusion had a flutter to it like a TV that was about to go off.

It was funny because, up to that point in time, the goat/shirt/towel had mostly irritated me, and now here I was, fearing I might lose the connection with this phantom of my own mind. I looked at the towel intensely, wanting to see a goat. There he was in the towel, but the whiteness of the towel made this goat seem ghostly and ephemeral. I panicked and caught my breath, thinking that something important was slipping away from me. The emotions of regret, dismay, and remorse filled me and caught in my throat.

The laughter did not come from the towel/goat, but it didn't come from me either. I saw in that instant that maybe there really was magic.

"Where were you going just now?" asked the goat/towel.

"Oh," I said, "I thought you had left or were thinking of leaving, and I wanted to hear the secret you referred to earlier."

"Well, that's no problem," said the towel/goat, "but first I have to tell you that it's quite impossible to leave yourself."

"Okay," I said, "so what's this secret you have that you were going to tell me?"

"Oh, that's no big thing," said the towel/goat. "I'm sure, if you thought about it, you'd realize it for yourself. It's just that the universe is trying to tell you things."

"What kind of things?" I asked.

"Mostly it's solid things that will make your spirit endure," said the towel/goat. "Without breaking the rules, I'll give you some hints."

The voice of the towel/goat changed here and came from the towel on the floor. "Why do you think there are things like death and love, vegetables, and sugar? You live in a universe that tries to seduce you each and every day. To your credit, you keep on trying, but just as reason is the perfect tool for science, it's the wrong tool for navigating the imagination."

"Vegetables, seduction, and a universe trying to tell me things. What are you trying to sell me here?" I inquired.

"Just this," said the towel/goat. "You don't know what you are, and the universe is really trying to give you clues."

I looked hard at the towel on the floor. The goat looked back. If there is one lesson I learned that day, it was to always put your dirty clothing and towels in the hamper. I'm careful now not to talk to dirty laundry.

French

Red loved waking up and going outside on a warm spring day. It was like everything got verified by the very act of being. *Could things get any better?* thought Red.

That's why he was doubly stumped when one of his hens, Georgia, greeted him in the most unusual way. At first he didn't understand what was happening. Only by focusing and listening intently did he realize that Georgia was speaking to him in French. *What new kind of hell is this?* thought Red. He was dumbfounded. It was like these hens stayed up at night and had meetings to confuse and confound him.

Now people in general are usually surprised to learn that chickens can speak in different languages. Chickens speak a different language within their cluck-cluck-clucks or buc-buc-bucs. Chicken speak is such a universal language in and of itself. It's hard to describe the incredibly subtle and nuanced quality of chicken speak. It's why the UN, in its infancy, debated whether chicken speak should be introduced as a universal language. They eventually settled on Esperanto, but chicken speak was very much in the running initially.

The thing about chickens speaking in different tongues was always discouraged because chickendom was such an ethnocentric culture. It was not that they were intolerant of other species. Everything that ever happened of any note usually happened within the chicken society.

Now it was also true, in terms of language, Red had his own baggage. He had a definite redneck twang to his way of speaking. Most hens found it very endearing and charming. The larger truth, however, was that, in terms of language, Red was just a bit limited. He could understand everything around him fine, and his ability to communicate when complimented by his swagger and wing flapping was really quite extraordinary. I guess what I'm saying is that he was just not a Hamilton College graduate.

All of this was not Red's problem just then in that moment. He was confronted by one of his hens, who, for some unfathomable reason, was speaking to everyone around her in French. First of all, where did she learn the language? Second, why the hell was she speaking it anyway? I only put that there to show the intensity and conflict-ridden nature of Red's thinking as this was all unfolding. Some things make sense, and others don't. Georgia speaking French fell into the latter category.

Red started to consider all options. Was he on *Candid Camera*? Was Rocko the Mean Butterfly pulling one of his sadistic jokes on him? Was the singularity happening, and was this the first evidence of that? Red was really wracking his brain to figure out just what was happening here.

As usual in such a tight-knit community as the chicken coop, the other hens as well as all the other farm animals started to be effected by Georgia's behavior. Ruth, one of Red's other hens, started to pretend to speak Polish. It was easy to see that she had no command of the language, as she actually kept repeating the same phrases. Mable joined the party, speaking in Russian. Well, she didn't really speak Russian, but she did say everything with a Russian accent while still speaking in English. Red thought, *This is getting out of control. What will happen next? Maybe one of them will admit to being a Republican.* Things were getting crazy.

Interestingly this whole scenario continued to expand and take control of the henhouse. A lot of the other farm animals would wander over and listen to the jabberwocky in the henhouse. They said it was charming and different and was great entertainment. The pigs, who were very smart but somewhat limited in their communication skills, thought all these accents and different speaks were delightfully engaging. The cows seemed actually to be calmed and relaxed by the different sounds that the chickens were producing. The dogs just barked and barked at the sounds coming out of the henhouse, but everyone knew that was because they spent too much time with the feeding hands. The relationship of the feeding hands to language all the animals knew had been stunted years ago, and their sophistication in regards to language was damaged at best.

This was all very well and good, but it was not helping Red solve his mystery. He wanted things back to the way they used to be—hens that clucked and all these international languages just a faraway reality that he didn't have to trip over. While the hens were in the yard socializing, Red took the opportunity to go into the chicken coop for some private time. He needed to be alone so he could think. He started to pace back and forth in the small coop, and then there before him, he saw it. We say our jaw dropped, but they say their beak melted. It's just an expression.

What Red saw on the floor of the coop was a newspaper article in French about France, and it was right in front of Georgia's nest. The feeding hands had put down some newspapers to warm the coop in wintertime, and there they were still doing much more than their job.

Red stood over the article and laughed. He finally understood where Georgia had gotten the idea of speaking French from. It was all a simple case of information being put before an intelligent, impressionable creature. The days of trying to figure out this mystery fell off Red's back. He clearly saw the whole recent happening with totally clarity.

Standing there on top of this newspaper story, Red felt a different feeling overtake him. Suddenly all the frustration and angst Red had wrestled with was right there in his body. Red had sharp talons. In a moment he said, "I cannot really remember."

Red lashed out at this newspaper below him and slashed it and tore at it with a ferocity worthy of a samurai warrior. He completely destroyed that article and, in truth, some of the floor underneath it. There was nothing left of the French article.

Things gradually returned to normal, but it took a long time. Red played the whole thing down. He dismissed the different attempts at languages and became ever more ardent in playing his rooster role. He was describing something they had always done in his quaint redneck chicken speak in a very loud voice when Rocko the Mean Butterfly flew overhead.

Rocko, hearing it, thought, *You can take the chicken out of the country, but you can't take the country out of the chicken.*

Red, for his part, saw Rocko and thought misguidedly, *Wow, he doesn't have to deal with stuff like this.*

A Post in the Ground

I want to tell you what happened last Tuesday and the events that flowed from it in the following days in the barnyard. Now of all events great and tiny and large and small, this one probably comes under the heading of insignificant. I won't qualify it any further, but needless to say, you don't have to document this under the heading of important. However, it did gather the attention of all the animals in the vicinity, and for that reason, I found it to be a notable event to record and pass on to you because I know your deep interest in the happenings of the barnyard and surrounding area.

Last Tuesday when everyone was somewhat in a very relaxed mood, Denise, one of Red's hens, came running into the barnyard and announced, "There is a post in the ground!"

Some proclamations turn everyone's heads, and they take notice. Perhaps it may have an effect on something in their lives. This pronouncement, in fact, did not have such an effect. Most of those in the surrounding area looked at Denise as if to say, "And why are you telling us this?"

I don't know if you remember, but Denise is not one to be ignored. The very excitement in her body had won the moment. She had attained a beachhead of enthrallment even as those around pretended a lack of fascination. This often happens to all of us. We feign a lack of interest even as our curiosity swells to bursting.

"A post in the ground?" someone said to Denise. And this was the breach in the dam. "Where is the post?"

"Down behind the barn, a little beyond the pigpen," said Denise.

"Hum!" said one of the geese. "Maybe it's there to measure something."

"That's what I thought," said Denise. "But what?"

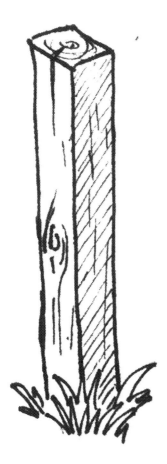

"I don't know," said the goose. "Maybe it's a marker for a new superhighway," she said tongue in cheek.

As comments go, this was a very unfortunate one. A goat was listening to this conversation, and they are entirely incapable of understanding irony.

You have probably already guessed what happened next. An unfounded rumor spread through the barnyard that a major highway was going to be built next to the pigpen. Now it's hard to say exactly who got this rolling because everyone knew enough not to take the goat's story seriously. I think it might have been one of the pigs who, when he heard about the superhighway, thought it was so funny that he took to repeating the story for the attached humor, not realizing that some of the other animals would not understand the joke.

As you might well imagine in such a tight-knit social community, the rumor took hold, and the belief was established that a superhighway was going to be built just there next to the pigpen. Now as if to verify the reality of this fact, everyone was directed to go look at the post in the ground, which was then used as some sort of proof that indeed a superhighway was coming through there. It was a strange reality to see everyone looking at this post in the ground and shaking their heads in affirmation about the story going round.

Now I just want to point out that, in actual fact, this phenomenon of the story of the highway was only believed by some of the more innocent and simple animals. Red the Rooster, the geese, and the pigs, for instance, found it amusing to push this story to its limit. The post in the ground and the superhighway became a sort of Santa Claus story that some of the more intelligent animals played with to carry along some of the simpler animals in a fantasy of the future.

It created then a scenario where these animals would discuss the highway in the presence of the goats or others who were more gullible in a way to entertain themselves and reinforce the fantasy of the building of this ghost highway. Now it's always true that, for every action, there is a reaction. In this particular case, the story of the highway became the cause. The effect was that some of the goats and other animals began to get ready to move. They could just not see themselves living in the middle of a superhighway.

This came to the attention of Red the Rooster and some of the geese while the pigs just thought it very funny that the goats were getting ready to move. Red went around and suggested it was time for truth regarding the post in the ground.

"I agree," said Pluto, a big, fat pig. (There's no insult intended. He was a big, fat pig.) "What is the truth of the post in the ground?"

"Gosh, you're right," said Red. "We still don't know why that post is in the ground. It's just important to not stress out these simple animals with this story that makes them think they're going to have to move."

"I agree," said Pluto. "Let's tell them it's a hitching post for the new bull that is going to join the barnyard in a little while."

It was quite a long and heated discussion, but finally all the animals who had pushed the highway story agreed that the post had a new purpose. It was where the bull, a new addition to the barnyard, would be stationed.

One of the goats became concerned that vehicles would run over the bull if they didn't move the post away from where the highway was going in. It took some time and patience to explain that there was no highway and that particular story had been a creation of some of the animals in the barnyard. Repetition, reassurance, and retraction of the original story finally won the day. Red knew they had accomplished the switch in stories once he heard some of the goats joking about how silly the highway idea was.

Now it's always true that fabrication creates the need for more fabrication. It's another way to say that lying creates the need for more lies. They wanted to know the name of the new bull. When would he be coming? What was his mother's maiden name? They were all burning questions, and curious minds wanted to know. The cows, however, asked the most pertinent question. They understood the post in the ground would tether him. But where was his stall going to be?

Red, of all the animals, stumbled over this question, and his lack of authority on the issue created a grey curiosity on the subject. The animals who had agreed to this untruth initially felt on shaky ground. Their collective reflex was to stop answering the onslaught of questions from the other barnyard animals. Their silence created a vacuum of belief and the loss of the storyline. Paradoxically this created more interest in the post in the ground.

Denise was back asking the ever-pivotal question, "What's the post in the ground for?"

It seemed to Red, the geese, and the pigs that the joke had turned on them. They retreated deeper into silence in the face of all these honest questions. Gradually after quite a bit of time, the serenity of the barnyard returned, dragging the post-in-the-ground question as a substantial sea anchor along with it. The survey crew for the new highway had come and gone without anyone much taking notice.

The Lovesick Donkey

There's a new arrival in the barnyard. It's a young donkey named Henry. He's actually very cute, and he was finding his way around quite nicely in the beginning. I draw your attention to Henry because he has fallen for the large mare who has been the farm workhorse for years. Now love is that thing that supposedly makes you blind to any faults in your beloved. The attraction happened immediately when Henry met Mildred the Mare.

I just want to paint you a picture of the incongruity involved here. Mildred is about eight times the size of Henry. I won't even bother to mention the differences in strength. It's a one-way David and Goliath love story. Mildred totally ignores Henry and goes about her daily activities without not so much as a nod in his direction. Henry is so memorized by Mildred that he has been seen walking into walls watching her as she passes by.

I guess reason can't understand the language of the heart in Henry's case. He appears to be a total prisoner of his adoration for Mildred. At first, since Henry was new to the barnyard, everyone just thought he was a goofy young donkey. His behavior seemed eccentric and odd, but then everyone realized that he only behaved that way when Mildred was nearby.

The other animals realized that Henry couldn't eat when Mildred was around. He was just too busy staring at her. He was, as they say, moonstruck. He began to follow Mildred around and, quite frankly, became a social awkward in his behavior to everyone else. He either ignored you or wanted to talk about Mildred.

Even though he was new to the barnyard, his information gathering focused totally around Mildred. He could not get enough information about her, and after a little bit, all the other animals became tired and weary of his excessive obsessive behavior focused totally toward Mildred. It became the new normal. Henry lived in a pool of unremitting, unrestrained, unruly, and unrequited love. He had created his own universe and was living within it with a commitment that can only come from the heart.

Now it's sort of interesting to note the other animal's reactions to Henry. I heard some geese say that Henry had eliminated the need to negotiate with the significant other. They commented how his obsequious behavior toward Mildred had become a very lonesome love dance indeed.

"Why? What do you mean?" asked a swan within hearing distance to this conversation.

"Love draws you deeper into the community," said the goose, "when there is a response from your beloved. If not, then you descend into isolation and narcissism."

I also overheard some of the goats talking about Henry's infatuation, and they seemed to think he just had terrible eyesight and saw Mildred as his equal. They started to call him "Hanky Panky, the Blind Donkey." They thought that rhymed and was terribly clever. Every time one of them passed Henry in the yard, he or she'd say the little rhyme and all laugh at their very sagacious witty playfulness.

The cows were actually very interesting on this subject and did not venture an opinion until I asked them about their new neighbor, Henry.

Bossie, an old-timer who had that name for years and said it was just fine with her, asserted, "Henry was a damn fool and should know better than to behave that way. What could one expect from an ass. They are a stupid, silly, obstinate animal."

Two of the pigs, Onion and George, were having a discussion about Henry when I approached them. They said, "It's just good entertainment for the old, boring barnyard."

"Besides," said George, "maybe it's a good thing to see someone reach for the unattainable. It gives these lowlife loafers around here something to think about. Maybe they'll start to see more to life than the next feeding."

Onion, who was always shocked by George's ideas, slowly shook his head and said he hadn't thought about that.

It was always interesting when a subject galvanized the barnyard and everyone had an opinion about it. I wanted to find Red the Rooster and get his take on the topic. I walked down toward the chicken coop with the hope of finding him.

He saw me coming, and before I could pose any questions, he asked me what I thought about sanctimonious morality. I was caught off guard and stuttered a stupid reply.

Trying to be cute, I said, "If the shoe fits?"

Red laughed. "One of your famous film makers said, 'The heart wants what the heart wants.'"

Red continued, "You were coming to ask me about Henry. Everyone has been talking about him, and opinions about him have been flying everywhere. I initially thought he was an embarrassment to himself and the barnyard until I had a conversation with Rocko the Mean Butterfly. Rocko said that love is the black hole of emotions. I asked him what he meant by that.

"He said love is one of the most powerfully defining emotions. The way it works is that, when someone experiences love, they surrender their identity to the other. Never mind if the love is not returned, although it's more powerful, creative, and dramatic if the other returns it. In that total capitulation of the heart, a space is created for a new identity to form. In that is the power of love.

"Wow" said Red, "is that what Henry is doing".?"

"Yes" said Rocko, ". Then he said the beauty of the process is that it doesn't take exceptional intelligence, creativity, or skill. It just needs a heart that is open to the world and wants what love can give.

"I asked what that was. And Rocko said that's like asking how far is infinity. All things are possible with love. What happens is that the lover and the object of love merge in the identity of the lover, and with that new identity, the lover goes back to love again. It's always the process of addition for those who dare to love. The identity of the lover grows until he has a special window to understand the universe."

Just then Mildred came out of the barn and headed down toward the meadow. Sure enough, right behind her came Henry with his mooneyes. I don't know if it was an illusion or if the sun was in my eyes, but it looked like Henry's hooves were not touching the ground. In that moment I envied him intensely.

A few of the goats saw Henry following Mildred and let loose with their predictable line. "There goes Hanky Panky, the Blind Donkey."

And they all started to giggle. It was another interesting day in the barnyard.

Harold the Leaf

It was autumn. The first hint of winter had arrived. There was a coldness in the air, and the leaves were all turning. The air had a dryness and feel to it that only the fall can bring. Way high up in the tree, in the back of the feeding hands' house, was a maple leaf named Harold. I'd like to tell you the story of Harold, but in order to do that, I have to back up a bit. Let me start by going all the way back to the end of last winter.

The frozen ache of winter was receding. Movement is life, and it started deep inside this maple tree. There were all the natural things of sap beginning to run and all of that. There was another mysterious movement also. The tree began to stretch in the promise of coming warmth. A thousand tiny, wooden fingers reached out to the sky where this promise came from. Who could say where it was located, but inside this monolith was a gladness of the coming spring.

Harold was then just a premonition of coming things. The trail by which he would arrive was being prepared. At this point he was unaware of his role in the occurring grand event. Time was on the side of the tree. It waited and grew in sync with the tumultuous weather swirling all around it. I don't think it's a stretch of the imagination to say it loved the million hints it got from the air and soil around it. It regained all those old relationships with its surroundings that winter had stolen from it for the last five months.

Weeks passed, and what began as a tiny ditty inside the tree turned into an aria. Life said yes to everything around it. Harold was a tiny, emerging bud. Encased in a sheathing that protected him from the cold, he began to yearn for freedom. Now who can say how all this happens, but the chick emerges from the egg, and Harold came out of his bud. The heavens erupted into joyous gladness at these events.

At first it was an incident onto itself. Tiny and frail, the green nodule tested the air. It had its own part to play in the song. There was no rushing this. It was just that the tree was pushing and the heat of the heavens was pulling. Harold knew even then that he was the center of the universe. He wanted to play his part. Slowly and almost imperceptibly, he unfolded his wings. Still only a promise of what they would become, the leaf began to spread out. Small and curled upon itself, it invited the air around it to tease it open.

Like a million years before, everything worked, and Harold became a leaf. At first it was slow and careful, but slowly as the days of spring passed, Harold took the nutrients from the tree and the magic from the sun and became a healthy, green leaf. Stretching, growing, and becoming aware of his companions around him, Harold sang the song of spring. He knew even then that he was fulfilling a promise to the world. How could he not be full of joy and happiness?

Harold looked around and saw that, whereas he was not at the top of the tree, he was very high up and to one side of his parent. The sun was relentless in giving what he wanted. Days passed. He experienced the rain, and it washed him. The dust from the air was washed away, and he could breathe deeply from the clear, beautiful air all around him. The storm of rain left, and the winds came. The winds thrashed him about, and it tested his ability to hang on to the tree. At the height of the windstorm, he felt the community of leaves around him.

Each day brought a new experience, and gradually summer arrived. He settled into a pattern of knowing. It became hotter, and the activity inside the tree increased until he could feel his part in all of it. It made him feel important and useful. The leaf that was Harold became strong, mature, and capable. He understood that he was only a small part in a larger thing, but without him, the larger thing could not happen.

The days of summer passed as they always do without much notice. Harold danced with the rain, wind, and song within. He was very happy to be a leaf. He could not imagine being anything else. In the heat of the long summer days, the engine that he was part of pumped the juice of life into his parent, and he was glad. In the summer nights, he rested and listened to the billions of sounds that came to him there way above everything.

Time passed as it always does, and there was a hint of a snarl in some of the clouds above. Cold weather would come again. At first it was just some of the nights where the cold crept in and lurked about. Harold stayed safe way up in the tree, away from this crawling predator. Eventually, however, it gained ground and touched Harold like he'd never been touched before. The change was magical and surprising.

Harold slowly became a work of art. The change was gradual and painless. He experienced this transition like it was a graduation. He had been part of a large machine, and now he was being called to become something all by himself. His green color faded, and he mysteriously took on some amazing colors. Harold watched as all the leaves around him made the same transition. Now they danced in the wind with an arrogance of beauty. It was not incorrect to say that Harold was glad and proud of what he had become.

The entire tree was a blossom of color and a perfect reflection of the face of God. It shouted out to anything with eyes, "Look at me."

The cold continued, however, its relentless march. Harold watched as some of his comrades left. He hung on, preferring to dangle in the increasingly chilled air. The days and night grew colder, and Harold realized it became harder and harder to hang on to the tree.

On one day in a slight breeze, which never would have worried him before, Harold let go. The fall to the ground was an eternity of floating. The air kissed and massaged him all the way to the ground. Harold was surprised to find there that he had become part of a larger canvas. He lay there, glad again to be part of something bigger. Gradually and slowly, Harold fell asleep.

Now I have a confession to make. I made up this story. I guess I was just tired of reporting the hard-hitting news from the barnyard and wanted to describe something just a bit whimsical to you. I tell you this because I don't want you to think I'm crazy enough to actually think that a leaf has feelings and thoughts.

The other part of that is that I don't want a story that is actually fantasy to encroach upon your belief in the reality of the news from the barnyard. I know the difference between reality and the unreal, and I just didn't want you to get confused by a silly story like this. I'll get back to reporting the hard news from the barnyard next time.

Brown Eggs

The curious thing about happiness is that it's like health. When you've got it, a lot of the time you don't know how lucky you are. That, however, was not the case with Red. He knew he was happy. He felt it in his chest, legs, and wings, but everything was cooperating to tell him that this was a great day and he was happy.

He was strutting about the barnyard, keeping tabs on things when he overheard two of his hens, Lucy and Marlene, discussing how Mable only laid brown eggs. He didn't think much of it. I mean, for all his measure, white, brown, or polka dot, they were all good eggs, and the feeding hands always collected them all. Nothing could take the edge off his good feelings today.

Later when he was standing by the entrance to the chicken coop, when the hens were returning to their roosts for the night, he saw that Mable was visibly upset. Red always looked into his hens' lives to assure that everything was okay. He went over to Mable's roost and discreetly asked her if there was anything wrong. In a tearful voice, Mable described how Lucy and Marlene were describing her as a lowlife because the eggs she laid were brown.

Red's initial reaction was to laugh, and he told Mable, "That's silly. Why, Ruth's eggs were also brown, and Denise's eggs were even slightly speckled."

Little did he realize it, but Red had just set up the lines of conflict for a hen fight that would nearly drive him to wish he were a goat. Not that there is anything wrong with goats. But if I may just for a moment interrupt this tragic story to philosophize about the nature of any creature's product. We are all in some way created by what we produce. In addition it's not unreasonable to be somewhat proud of that product. Now if this is turned in the opposite direction and we are made to feel bad about that product, it's an intriguing thing that the very thing that buoyed us up before can now act as an anchor to pull us down. It makes one wonder which is more powerful: the egg or what we think about the egg.

These ruminations were not the thing on Red's mind just now. As always, he was zeroing in on what was developing in front of him. The chicken coop had a problem, and he was going to try to fix it. I'll cut to the quick and tell you what happened so you don't have to listen to all the messy details as they developed.

Lucy and Marlene joined forces with Georgia, and the three of them besmirched the eggs of Mable, Ruth, and Denise. It was a chicken fight. They said terrible things about each other that were totally unrelated to the eggs, and it seemed to Red that they just liked being mean to each other.

One funny aside to this whole thing was that Denise was sort of a scatterbrain, and she would forget the conflict and approach Lucy, Marlene, and Mable. She would greet them as if she were their best buddies. She just liked everybody. That was until she was reminded that her precious eggs had been gored. Then she was all elbows and assholes. Marlene, Mable, and Lucy would run for cover because, as jovial and nice as Denise could be, she could also be sort of foul-mouthed and nasty.

It was developing into a real war zone, and Red took note that the first casualty of this war was his happiness and peace of mind. Red had protocols to deal with situations like this. First he explained in a very calm and reassuring voice the total absurdity of trashing each other's eggs. This was usually followed by a strong rooster march, accompanied by crowing and wing flapping that was truly impressive. Next he took the high roost in the chicken coop and indulged long and hard in stern looks all the way round. This dampened things down dramatically, and anyone observing this command performance had to admit that Red the Rooster was in total control.

The wind blows a leaf, and it is in control to the degree that it follows where the wind blows. Now this unfortunately was essentially the measure of Red's control in this situation. It was not apparent at first as the hens all acted subservient and acknowledged Red's leadership. The thing was, however, hens, while ruled by their rooster, are driven by their nature. That nature was liking the fight that was brewing. Perhaps a better way to say it was there was no rooster or authority on the field of battle. Those brown or speckled eggs had to be dealt with. The silent drums of war called powerfully to these hens.

Red's happiness drained away like a child's balloon a day after the birthday. Red followed his problem through his failures and into the giddy excitement of the hens' need for conflict. He was, after all, the rooster. He took the good with the bad, and that day didn't need a label for him to know that it was bad. Red also knew, when things were pulled from his talons, away from his control, the next thing to do was watch. So Red watched as the hens treated each other terribly over the color of their eggs. Now Mable, Ruth, and Denise were slamming the white eggs of Lucy, Marlene, and Georgia.

Red could see the silliness of the whole thing, and it reminded him of a historical conflict he had heard about from the land of Lilliput. There two countries had also gone to war over eggs. In that conflict, it was the issue of which end an egg should be opened on. That war, Red thought, had at least some merit, whereas the conflict he was refereeing seemed to him totally without any redeeming quality. Now while he was not sophisticated enough to have an opinion about which end of an egg to open. He did feel in his gut that the outside color of an egg was not important. Inside all opinions lies another reason. In truth, the other reason lying behind Red's public thought was that he loved all his hens and was very sad to see them engaged in such a conflict.

All conflict is change; all change keeps coming. And Red watched and learned. The eggs were an excuse for a thought that did not matter, and soon the hens tired themselves out over this silly argument. It took quite a while, but slowly it went away. In tiny increments, things returned to normal. They had measured the other and themselves in the process. After the psychological bath of war, they wanted peace. It was Lucy, Marlene, and Georgia who first apologized. There were no winners, and that worried Red just a bit. He knew he would keep his ears open for any comments about the color of eggs in the future. Sometimes no one wins; chickens just get tired of fighting for a while.

Becoming Part of the Problem

As usual, I went over to the barnyard to see what was happening. I was sort of pleased and intrigued to find everyone there content and happy. Being the ardent reporter that I am, I asked a lot of questions to see if there were anything afoot that would be worthy of reporting to you. I guess I irritated some of the barnyard animals. So as it turns out the story, this week is about a backlash from the barnyard.

Indeed that might be a rather inaccurate way of describing what happened. You see, if left to their own devices, the animals in the barnyard actually live a quiet and stoic existence. They get up in the morning when Red crows and eat. They commune with each other, and they navigate the uncertainties of the day with calm forbearance. This is really all to their credit and speaks well of their collective barnyard culture.

I suspect I might have inserted an unnecessary ripple in this serenely floating wave of their social fabric. You see, I've always found something there of import to report. I don't think I've ever allowed myself to exaggerate or misquote anyone. I've tried to focus on what was simply happening. I just want to qualify my side of this story before you are bombarded by the facts from my detractors as it were. This is difficult to report because I've become part of the story here, and as you well know, that makes impartiality more difficult.

The other side to this rather intriguing episode is that I'm the voice for these guys. I document what happens and what is said, and I have to sometimes translate various animal languages into the document before you now. It's just that sometimes the perpetrators of these various actions can take issue with how they are characterized. I don't truly know if this was the unconscious resentment underneath the affair I'm about to describe here in its most accurate detail.

As it happened, I was asking a small sheep if anything frightened her last week. The ram took issue with that question, and I immediately apologized. His reaction was based on the fact that a young animal can be shooed into fear by the simple suggestion that there is fear to be afraid of. I understood that and reconfigured my question in more banal terms. Did anything happen to you last week that you remember or want to tell me about? To my surprise, that also irritated the ram.

I quickly agreed that my questions were a bit intrusive because the ram outweighed me by forty pounds. Now I like to think I would have agreed with him anyway because the last thing I want is to scare young, developing minds. Either way, the issue became moot when a duck that was passing by quacked an annoying comment about me asking stupid questions again. There were some goats on the outskirts of hearing distance from this conversation, and they immediately joined a chorus of complaints about my investigative work.

I've always thought that silence is the language of the gods, so I retreated post haste when this collective voice began to rail at me. Now I know that goats will join any group just for the momentary feeling of belonging. I figured I would outwait them. *Ten minutes tops*, I thought, *and their anger would be a fading memory.* What I did not count on was Onion the Pig, who was walking by and becoming one of my detractors. Onion got his name because he loves to eat onions, and if you doubted this, all you have to do is smell his breath.

Onion said that usually he didn't agree with goats on anything, but in this case, they were dead on right. Turning to me, he said, "You always come to the barnyard and tell stories about us and then describe the negative side of the barnyard. We don't exist in order to become the narrative for someone else's entertainment. We are barnyard animals who have dignity and merit all by ourselves. Placing us as characters in a moron's stories is degrading and insulting."

I had really managed to hold my tongue until the point that a pig called me a moron. "Now just a second," I said. "First of all, I only report the truth as I objectively see it."

"That's it, mutton head," said Onion. "It's how you see it. Don't you see that we animals don't need a narrative in order to exist like you feeding hands types do?"

I stuttered to a stop. I was a bit over my head and didn't know how to respond to that last comment. "Look!" I said. "Why don't I get Red the Rooster and Rocko the Mean Butterfly to listen to both sides of this debate? I'll do whatever they decide."

"Fine," said Onion. "But I think we should invite everyone from the barnyard and the meadow to listen and have input."

"Great," I said, mostly because I didn't know what else to say. This also gave me the excuse to depart temporarily. "We will meet here tomorrow and present the arguments before Red and Rocko."

The next day, I arrived early and waited while all the animals drifted together for the presentations. I just want to honestly report there was some heckling while the group gathered.

A swan yelled out, "Hey, idiot, why don't you check your watch to see what time it is?"

The animals always make fun of the feeding hands for having machines to tell them what time it is. They all know that it is now. I'm just stating for the record that the crowd was actually quite hostile because they all laughed when I did check my watch.

Red and Rocko arrived and took very unassuming positions, considering they would be the arbitrators in all of this. Red sat atop a fence post, and Rocko sat on a low-hanging tree limb. They listened with intense concentration as Onion and some of his pig brothers made the case that I was an intrusive, slow-witted, meddling ninny who told stories of questionable merit about the barnyard animals. In addition they said animals didn't need to depend on a story to verify or reify their existence.

It was my turn to talk. I explained how I always tried to be objective and honest in relating how I saw things or explained the happening in the wild or barnyard. I continued to explain my side of the issue and was quite eloquent, if I have to say so myself.

Now that both the pigs and I had our public say, Red and Rocko retreated into the barn for a private conference. They emerged quite quickly, and Rocko spoke for the both of them when they returned.

"First of all," he said, "the name-calling was somewhat appropriate; however, the barnyard animals have overstepped their boundaries by objecting to the stories, but not for the reason they thought. It's a good thing that stories are told about the animals because the feeding hands needed constant guidance, which they could only get from observing and hearing about how the animals conducted themselves."

They encouraged me to continue to document the affairs as best I could of all the animals in the vicinity. It was their hope that someday the feeding hands might learn something from these stories.

I could see that ol' onion breath didn't like that. Ha!

Rocko Taunts the Swallow

I think it was William Blake who said, "The road to excess leads to the palace of wisdom." I couldn't help remembering that quote when I overheard Rocko the Mean Butterfly describing the pleasure, enchantment, and excitement of flying. The way he was describing it made it sound like an adventure in risk. I've noted many times that his descriptions of ordinary things he does every day sound to me like a confrontation with high adventure.

Perhaps that's just the way butterflies live. I'm not really sure, but I do recognize that listening to his tasks of daily living sound to me like someone living on the edge or very close to it. I'm sure I won't do it justice, but I will try to recount a description he gave of avoiding a swallow who was trying to make of him a lunch and how he not only avoided this predator but turned it into a playful game. I'd like to additionally note that I tried to get Rocko to repeat this description for the record, but he declined, saying it was not at all noteworthy.

Rocko was out in the meadow down behind the barn when he became aware that a swallow had keyed in on him as a possible meal. He said a butterfly can tell when this happens because there are these conduits of energy forethoughts. I'm not really sure what that means, but he said, as a butterfly, you can feel where the attack will come from. He described glancing in that direction and saw a rather young swallow had singled him out. He described laughing to himself and decided to have some fun with the whole situation.

He retained his position of prominence on top of a large flower he had been obtaining pollen from and waited for the swallow to make his move. Now as almost everyone knows, a swallow has the ability of incredible flying speed. Rocko, in telling this story, said he was counting on this. He waited for the swallow to strike, and just with the right timing, he slid down to the stem of the flower, pulling the face of the flower into the swallow's flight path.

He said the crash of the swallow into the flower was comical. He hit the flower, and it made him, the swallow, and the flower bend way over as the speed of the bird was transmitted into the flower. The stem of the flower was like a bungee cord, and once it maxed out on the downward direction, it rebounded, throwing the bird out into the air again. The bird thought it had just misjudged its attack and tried to recover during the rebound.

Rocko, who had planned this event and maintained his grip on the flower, now released his hold and fluttered away from the flower, trying to look clumsy and like an easy target. This encouraged the swallow to continue his attack. The bird was attempting to fly against the movement the flower had sent him in and was actually working very hard to gather forward movement. During this split second, Rocko was fluttering just out of reach, looking very vulnerable and helpless.

The swallow regained his flying posture and dove toward Rocko. The bird flew into a spiderweb that Rocko had lifted into place as Rocko fell out of the bird's attack path. The surprise of this almost invisible barrier disrupted the bird's flight path, and he also fell as he was caught off guard by this dainty defense. He landed a bit away from Rocko and immediately cleaned off the ethereal web from his wings. He looked over and saw that Rocko was flopping on the ground like he was helpless. The instinct of the predator was triggered, and he immediately began to hop toward Rocko. Just as the bird reached striking distance, Rocko lifted into the leaves just above him and blended into the foliage. The swallow thought he knew where Rocko had entered the foliage and dove recklessly into the leaves at that point.

The leaves provided multiple hiding places for Rocko, and he tantalized the swallow by showing the tip of his wings behind a leaf. The swallow found nothing when he charged that particular leaf, only then to see more bait behind a different leaf. This cat-and-mouse routine continued until the swallow flew out of the foliage, exasperated at his inability to corner the butterfly. Only then did he realize that Rocko was clinging to his back and riding him like a bucking bronco.

Now almost everyone knows that swallows retaliate in groups when they sense they are being threatened. Having Rocko on his back and being unable to dislodge him qualified in this swallow's mind as a threat. He flew back to his nesting area in the barn and signaled to his cronies the nature of the attack upon him. The other swallows rose to his defense and found nothing. Rocko was gone and thought he was quite clever to have humiliated this young swallow before his peers.

It did remain a mainstay of the swallow stories in the nesting area of how the young swallow had called for help against the invisible butterfly. Rocko's appraisal of his actions was that he had given an education to another animal. The young swallow, however, reinforced the tag by which Rocko was known, the Mean Butterfly. Indeed there was a consensus among the animals that heard this story that Rocko's lesson to the swallow was just a bit on the mean side of things.

This started a debate as to how and why you move from excess to the palace of wisdom. Did Rocko or, for that matter, Blake know something from ordinary events that built a bridge to loftier ideas? Some of the pigs said it was the swallow's motive of hunger that was sabotaged and translated into highfalutin thoughts by Rocko that allowed the entrance into the palace. A nearby goose said no. It was the intriguing dance of defiance by Rocko in the face of danger that allowed entrance into the palace.

A small, quiet voice spoke from the bushes where this debate had been taking place. It was a praying mantis who had a difficult dialect and soft voice, but the culture of the barnyard encouraged her opinion. She said after a somewhat awkward translation, "That entrance into the palace of wisdom came from the willingness to play even before any thought in the face of death and danger."

The animals that had gathered together for this debate looked over and saw that Rocko nodded and showed a slight smile as the praying mantis finished her contribution to this discussion.

A nearby goat asked, "Where is this palace? Can we go visit it?"

"No!" said Red the Rooster, who had been listening to the conversation. "They don't allow goats there," he said, tongue in beak.

The Sea Rescue 15

Now I'm not sure this is actually a legitimate Red and Rocko story. It's because Rocko heard it from a sailor when he was flying down next to the docks. And to complicate things even more, I heard it from a goat who overheard it when Rocko told Red the Rooster about it. So really take this with a grain of salt. I'm just not sure how true this all is.

Supposedly the sailor told Rocko that the ship he was on capsized in a storm and all hands were thrown into the water and doomed. They didn't even have time to man the lifeboats as the ship went over in rough seas. The waves were like fifty feet high, and it was totally impossible to even try to swim in such seas. The sailor said, as he fell into the ocean and the ship rolled over onto its side, there was just no possibility of hope.

This is the point in the story where the goat might have exaggerated. He said the sailor told Rocko that, as he looked up, he saw more than a thousand butterflies making their yearly journey to Africa. He said they literally blocked out the sun. That's where I think he's exaggerating because it was a stormy day and the sun was probably not out anyway. Maybe that's not the most important part of the story, however. The sailor said there were about thirty some sailors in the water, and they were having a terrible time just keeping their heads above water at that point.

It stretches credulity, but the sailor told Rocko that the butterflies spread out in a large circular formation. The thing they did next is hard to believe, but supposedly they started to move their wings in unison and at a very rapid speed without moving in any direction. It had the effect of calming the ocean in a large area around the sailors. Most of the sailors were good swimmers, and given this advantage, they began to swim and look up at the butterflies.

The ship, which was partly caught in the becalmed area, was in the process of sinking. A group of butterflies broke off from the main formation, dove down toward the sinking ship, and landed on the uppermost side where the lifeboats were still tied in place. The butterflies landed on these lifeboats, and once the sailors saw that, they immediately swam over and began to climb up toward the lifeboats.

Now I guess it was a real race with time because the ship was taking on water rapidly, and the sailors were trying to climb up and untie these lifeboats so they could have some safety from the elements. They managed to get some of the lines loose as the ship began to slip toward its final resting place. The one lifeboat slipped free from the larger ship and fell into the ocean. Many of the sailors scrambled aboard. There was just one other sailor trying to free another lifeboat, and I guess he had a knife on him. And as the larger ship went under and took him and the lifeboat with it, he managed to cut the final lines holding it to the mother ship, and it bobbed up from the ocean like a cork half filled with water but separate at last from the doomed ship.

The sailors pulled the two boats together and began to bail the late arrival so it was usable. They then tied the two boats together, and there was enough room for all the sailors to have a place in one or the other of these lifeboats. They then tied the storm covers over both boats and hungered down to wait out the storm.

Before they closed the storm shields over the lifeboats, they looked up and saw the butterflies were breaking up their formation and gaining altitude. One of the sailors said he saw them as they flew out of sight, going east. Now according to the sailor, they were bounced around in the waves of that storm for about two more days. It finally let up, and they opened their storm covers and floated helplessly on the ocean for another seven days before a passing tramp steamer picked them up.

All thirty-two sailors survived. There had been thirty-three in the lifeboats originally, but one of the sailors died of the hiccups. Evidently he was allergic to saltwater, and it gave him a severe case of the hiccups. He passed away from them a day before being rescued. I guess that's the kind of horrible tragedies that happen on the high seas.

The sailors told their story to the authorities after being rescued, but they were not believed. The authorities just assumed they had been traumatized by their terrible experience at sea. They were all given sedatives and advised to take a long, restful vacation. Now when some of the sailors persisted in trying to tell the story of what had happened to them, they were put in small rooms, and men with white coats took care of them.

Now I know that sailors for centuries have told stories about sea monsters and various other sea creatures. This just didn't strike me as that kind of story. I know it sort of bends the mind into a weird shape and doesn't conform to what we think about the sea, butterflies, or weather. The thing is the goat said that Rocko said the sailor had a look in his eye when he told this story that spoke of adventures experienced and overcome. The goat said that Rocko said that there was still the shadow of fear conquered in the sailor's eyes as he told this tale.

I really don't know what to think, and I am in a quandary about relaying this story to you. I have been an accurate reporter, consistently telling the truth about what happens in the barnyard. I have never exaggerated or bent the truth at all. Now here in this situation where the information comes to us secondhand, I think we can reliably contest the details and truth of the story. This was my honest assessment of this story until I decided to ask someone who knows about such things.

I asked Red to set up a meeting with Rocko the Mean Butterfly. Initially Rocko was hesitant because he didn't have a high opinion of us feeding hands species. He finally agreed when it was conveyed that the purpose of the meeting was to determine the truth about the butterflies' rescue of the sailors at sea. We met under some large maple trees on a warm afternoon. Rocko was polite but formal.

I explained my problem with the hearsay quality of the story. I then also added the improbable nature of some of the details related in this story.

Rocko looked at me with sympathy in his small eyes. "Butterflies are small, but collectively we have the largest heart in the universe. Generally speaking, butterflies would prefer that you not know if that story is true or not because credit for love given takes some of the magic out of it."

So I guess, after talking to Rocko, I feel like it's okay to tell you the story and allow you to make your own decisions about it.

Rocko's Identity

It was one of those days where everything shouted out to you, "All's right with the world." Rocko the Mean Butterfly was going from flower to flower, enjoying his life with an intensity that was not really describable. The reason it's somewhat difficult to describe is because what he was doing is uniquely a butterfly's domain. Rocko was covered with the pollen from all these plants he was visiting as he enjoyed the nectar from them all. Now for feeding hands, that sounds rather banal, but I can assure you it was far from that.

The pollen tingled and vibrated these tiny hairs on a butterfly's wings while the nectar from each flower was akin to sampling in succession the finest cuisine in the world. Now this doesn't even begin to describe the wonderful feelings and sensations this flower hopping created for Rocko. Butterflies go into a state akin to satori when they flower-hop. There is no other animal that has such a natural venue to bliss as the butterfly except the feeding hands, but that doesn't count because they, the feeding hands, don't use the plants that would do that for them. They have made them illegal.

That's just a bit off topic, however, and as we return to Rocko's thoughts, they are clear and lucid, being abundantly lubricated by these wonderful natural flowers. Inside that cathedral of internal beauty, Rocko had an interesting thought. *It doesn't seem right that they call me the Mean Butterfly*. This thought occurred against the backdrop of what Rocko was experiencing. Beauty, courage, wisdom, and character built atop concise and logical thinking were the foundations to Rocko's identity.

Now he remembered the different stories that built his reputation, for example, the time he taunted the rhinoceros to charge and flew up just in time for the rhino to knock himself out on the large boulder behind him. He remembered how rude that large, smelly creature had been to him and how the rhinoceros deserved that lesson. He remembered how he had humiliated the large tiger in the jungle by getting him to jump at him while he fluttered over a water hole. The other animals laughing had finished that job for him. He remembered how he had spooked an elephant herd to trample a bunch of laughing hyenas. Those obnoxious creatures had mostly gotten out of the way.

He understood why everyone might think him a bit mean after this type of behavior, but after thinking about it, he simply thought he had bested various opponents in what he considered fair contests. It was not right. Why didn't they call him Rocko the Good Fighter, Rocko the Clever, or even Rocko the Agile? He simply thought they were focusing on the wrong aspect to this whole identity thing.

He thought perhaps it was because of the whole beauty thing. Thinking that a creature is beautiful many times denies all the other qualities that that creature possesses. It's a strange quality in the thinking mind. And Rocko knew that a lot of the other animals were not as advanced as the butterflies were when it came to thinking. Perhaps it was a reaction against that very beauty that allowed the other animals to slide into the definition of mean when it came to Rocko. He was, he had to admit, very beautiful.

Now the other thing about butterflies, Rocko realized, was their relationship to the wind. Nobody besides butterflies understood how that worked. And to really understand that phenomenon, you also had to understand just how tough and strong butterflies are. Everyone thought that butterflies were delicate. Ha! Can a delicate creature make an airborne journey over four thousand miles every year? The toughness and durability of a butterfly's ability to fly is better than anything the feeding hands had ever built, and there are rumors that they had built some impressive flying machines. The butterflies had no protection. It was the wind, the intuition of the butterfly, and the sky.

A butterfly catches a breeze and is lifted into a dance that is beautiful and different each time. The choreography of what happens between the wind and a butterfly is amazing enough to make God stutter. It is one reason why there is such a large depository of wisdom in butterflies. You simply can't have experiences like that without seeing beyond the veil itself. Life and death and joy and sadness are introduced in the vestibule of this experience. These were the musings of Rocko, and they also didn't seem to attach any quality of meanness to him. Why did everyone call him the Mean Butterfly?

One of the things Rocko liked about going from flower to flower was that it made him feel present. Now in this state of presence, he seemed to have a judgment about his thoughts that allowed him to subtract the bad thoughts from the good ones as it were. In this state of reverie, he realized an interesting thing. He was not responsible for what other creatures called him. It was his job to be himself, and as he reflected upon this, he thought he was very good at being himself.

Drunk with pollen and nectar, Rocko lifted up into a warm breeze and allowed the wind to roughly toss him about. It always cleared Rocko's thinking to meet his ever new, old friend this way. He let his invisible companion blow all his thoughts away. He fell back on relying on thousands of years of instinct. He was at home there in the sky.

Of a sudden, Rocko realized why they called him the Mean Butterfly. All creatures must protect themselves from the other. It's just the way they take ownership of their bodies. It really doesn't have much to do with the other, except that it excludes and protects him or her from the world of thought. In truth sometimes even that doesn't work.

Rocko decided to fly over and visit his old friend, Red the Rooster. Sometimes it's just good to have a friend to talk to.

Gloria and Winthrop

I just wanted to tell you about this very curious relationship between these two unlikely characters from the barnyard. Rocko the Mean Butterfly described the connection between these two. Winthrop the Earthworm and Gloria the Chicken have established a very curious relationship. Now Winthrop is actually quite an average earthworm in most respects. He has been doing earthworm stuff his whole life.

"Now what precisely is earthworm stuff?" you ask.

Most everyone knows that the earthworms aerate the soil by making trillions of tiny caves through the earth. What most no one knows about is the process that goes along with this effort by the earthworms. This interlocking labyrinth of tiny tunnels is a story of love. Now I know that sounds silly and strange, but let me for a minute just describe how these burrows are created.

There are billions and billions of these guys doing their work under our feet on this planet we call home. Now the most amazing thing about this is that, without them there, we wouldn't be here. They, along with some other guys in the soil, make it possible for the soil of this earth to grow plants. The final loop in this mystical circle is the animals including the feeding hands. They depend on the plants for their existence. So you see, these guys laboring diligently there in the soil create effects way beyond their initial intent. This, however, is only the most banal description of the effects of this relationship between Mother Earth and our wiggly friends.

There is a great difference between the description and the doing in most things. In this particular case, that difference crosses a dimension that is practically mysterious. In doing a job, sometimes the task becomes the world. This is not the case with the earthworms and their tunnels. I don't want to get too technical, but let me just for a moment try to describe this process from the vantage point of the earthworms. You see, the earthworms vibrate at a certain frequency when they dig. This vibration flows along the tunnel channel and combines with all the other worms working at the same time.

This quivering palpitation flows though the earth and unites the efforts of all the earthworms in a symphony that ricochets back to each digger. A scientist stumbling on this phenomenon might try to dissect it into logical parts and describe it so he can explain the practical results of these many workers. No one could fault his efforts, but the core and pith of his description would lack a certain valuable part. You see, this vibration sings a type of ecstasy to the bodies of these worms all digging at the same time that can only be described as love.

Someone watching a mother and child and trying to explain what's happening in scientific terms might miss the fundamental expression of what is being exchanged. This is what the scientist describing the relationship between the earth and the worms would miss. In simple terms, there is love in the relationship between the worms and the planet, and the worms know it when they dig.

Here in the story, Rocko laughed at the feeding hands' efforts to find other intelligent life out in the universe. "It's just there under their feet."

Now I know that most animals don't have a high opinion of earthworms, but this was not the case with Gloria, one of Red's hens. She loved earthworms. She felt herself lucky and happy to ever cross paths with an earthworm because she thought them the tastiest of treats. Gloria was an interesting hen because she was quite focused on her feeding efforts. The other hens had a nickname for Gloria because of the way she went about eating in the barnyard. Gloria would go out into the barnyard and look for things to eat on the ground. Her pecking was continuous and persistent, and nothing on the ground escaped her examination and pecking. Because of this, they called her pecker head, behind her back of course.

Now it was early one morning when a particularly heavy rain had chased Winthrop out of the topsoil. Earthworms come out of the ground when it becomes saturated with water so they can breathe more easily. The experience for the earthworms of the air environment is like a tantalizing taste of a drug. Winthrop, who had been digging but now experienced the air environment, watched as Gloria approached. He was feeling the afterglow of the ecstasy of digging with the drug effect of the air and thought maybe Gloria was coming to thank him for all his hard work.

You can well imagine his surprise when Gloria tried to turn out his lights with a staccato-like pecking attack that was relentless and almost deadly. Winthrop denied Gloria her treat because he was full of the glory and ecstasy of digging just then. He bent and dodged like a kung fu warrior. His defensive maneuvers were just enough to stay ahead of Gloria and off her dinner plate. The attack had surprised Winthrop, but once he parried Gloria's initial attempts at killing him, he felt confident that he could manage himself in this air environment.

Now Gloria, for her part, was not to be denied so easily. She saw her failure, and like most chickens in that situation, she circled the intended meal with an eye to figuring out a better attack. She scrutinized Winthrop like a piece of grain that had just outwitted her. Determination and hunger combined in her new attack made the next effort at eating Winthrop more ferocious and lethal. Winthrop, however, had warmed to this new game, and using the vibration of the very earth as his ally, he evaded Gloria's new efforts with ease.

This sparring effort went on and on. Gloria tried to enhance her diet while Winthrop tried to keep life and limb together. Gloria was nothing if not persistent. Winthrop, for his part, drew on the resources of this symphony that was a natural vibration in his very body. At this point in the story, Rocko insinuated that really there was no contest because Winthrop was using an energy that dwarfed the chicken coop culture.

This contest went on and on longer than I care to describe here. Suffice it to say, Gloria really exhausted herself, trying to peck at the ground where Winthrop had just been. Now as I've pointed out here, Gloria has her faults, but a lack of intelligence and imagination could not be assigned to her. She was an intelligent and fair-minded hen who always tried to keep an open mind about the world around her. At some point in this contest, it must have dawned on her that her adversary was also an intelligent and interesting creature.

Then at some point in this match, they began to exchange words. This, to make a long story short, led to entente. Stranger concordats have been made. Gloria and Winthrop became friends. The struggle of life and death between them became the cement that bound their relationship strongly together.

Winthrop always kept one eye open, however, as he said, "You'll never know when hunger will get the best of ol' pecker head."

Grover the Grub

I wanted to describe an animal from the barnyard. Technically I'm not sure he qualifies as a member of the barnyard. He was born there and has been living his whole life there, so I think he really is a member in good standing in the barnyard. His story brings a certain gravity to the barnyard. I just wanted to tell you Grover's story. Well, let me describe him and his relationships, and I'll let you be the judge.

He's Grover the grub, and he lives in the fence post next to the barn. Perhaps I should back up a bit and describe his arrival and early development. Grover's parent was a beetle who visited this very fence post in early spring. She laid some eggs there, and they developed into some larvae and finally matured into a grub. That's where we are catching up to Grover.

Now I know a lot of feeding hands do not have a high opinion of grubs. So before you pass judgment on Grover, let me just tell you a little about the beetle's place in the universe. Grubs are essentially the children of beetles, and beetles are God's favorite animal.

"How do you know that?" you ask.

It's easy because there are more different kinds of beetles here on earth than any other type of animal. It just stands to reason, if he made more different kinds of them, they must be his favorite animal.

Grover was very good at being a grub. He enjoyed it, and his heart sang the slow, murmuring, relentless grub song. It was not really a song, but rather a quivering oscillation of life itself. There was the wood, and inside of that the grain. And even then beyond that was the knots, rot, and pitch. His universe was varied and always a challenge. Grover had an intimate relationship with this fence post. It was his world, his universe, and his home.

Now even saying that, it was not like Grover was unaware of the rest of the barnyard. He could tell just from the vibration in the ground up through the fence post which animal was passing by. The horses sent a solid, strong thump that spoke to vigor, brawn, and muscle. The cows he felt as lumbering carefulness. The goats spoke of a hurried, myopic thoughtlessness. The sheep told of a quick pattern of relentless sameness.

The chickens were a quick, unpredictable strutting. The ducks liked to trick him by taking flight, but he could always tell it was them prior to that by their flapping waddle. The feeding hands were, of course, easy because they had that off-balance two-step. The geese and swans were difficult to tell apart just in their vibrations. He told them apart by the speed and canter of their gait. Actually as time went on, he could identify each individual in the barnyard from the vibration of his or her stride. It might not sound like a personal way to know another, but the truth is that our footfall says who we are. So in one sense, Grover knew everyone in the barnyard.

It was true, while Grover had identified everyone in the barnyard, it was probably honest to say that most of the animals there on the farm were not aware of his existence. Unfortunately that was not totally true. One steady visitor to the barnyard was intensely aware of Grover's existence. His interest in Grover revolved around the fact that Grover represented a high protein diet for him.

This was Wolf the Woodpecker. Wolf was not his given name, but everyone called him that because he would chase wolves through the low brush to stir up bugs from the surrounding flora. He had learned this trick as a young woodpecker when he realized he could dive-bomb other animals and send them into a panic. The wolves seemed especially susceptible to this strategy, and once he got them running, it was easy to follow along and reap the stirred-up insect population. His real given name was Walter.

Some grubs stay in this larvae stage for up to five years. Grover was not sure how much time had passed. Grubs have the happy task of living inside their meal. In order to move forward into the wood or tunnel they are creating, they have to eat their way there. They pack frass behind them. Frass is composed of fine sawdust and excrement that is left as they pass through the wood. A good comparison for us feeding hands would be to describe someone living inside a chocolate cake. It's just hard to keep track of time while you're doing that.

Anyway the day came when Wolf discovered the presence of Grover. Up to this point in time, Grover had been living in a utopia. His universe pampered and took extreme care of him. I don't speak woodpecker, so it's hard to know exactly how Wolf found out about Grover's existence. I can only speculate that it was due to some uncanny woodpecker trait that I am unaware of, or else he saw the sawdust from one of Grover's tunnels.

At first the attack was cautious and preliminary. Grover felt it like a machine gun firing at his house. Perhaps it was the scent of blood. Something was verified for Wolf, and all of a sudden, the attack increased in intensity. What began as an assault upon his house became personal and an attack upon him. Grover prayed for healthy wood to stay between him and the woodpecker. There was an intensely, unrelenting fast staccato pecking that had an incredible strength to it.

Life leaps forward to life and recoils from fear. Grover took deep drinks of the latter. The terror and destruction in this small world can only be compared to what it must have felt like on Iwo Jima or Guadalcanal. Hunkered down in what he had previously thought as a safe place, Grover now saw his world being ripped apart by a beast with an iron beak.

Grover knew every inch of this fence post, and he could tell from the intensity of the attack and his knowledge of the wood that he was in trouble. His one chance of saving himself depended upon him being able to go down three inches and over two in order to get behind a knot that just might give him some protection. The woodpecker's beak sent wood flying every which way. A certain anarchy to the attack created a total sense of pandemonium. Grover knew how fast he could move through this wood, and he knew his chances weren't good.

It's not like the fate of the world hung in the balance. There was, however, a struggle between life and death. There just are certain forces at work that we all recognize. The large prey upon the small, and strong prey upon the weak. And the sun comes up in the morning, and those who have not survived the struggle for life are just not there. Grover did not feel the sun warm his fence post that morning. Sometimes things happen, and that's just the way it is. There was no requiem for Grover. Wolf flew away with a smile on his beak. There are winners and losers, and that's just the way it is, even in a children's story.

Lenard and Jerry

I 'm sort of going back in time here. By that, I mean that this story happened quite some time ago, and the barnyard animals who were the main players in this strange tale are mostly long gone. I guess it really doesn't matter, but the memory of this narrative came to me when I saw two of our present occupants of the barnyard arguing over mostly nothing.

I didn't really remember this incident as much as I heard about it from the various animals I had interviewed over the years. I had gathered enough of the story to feel like I had some pretty accurate information about it. This story stuck in my head as one of those occurrences that are universal to anyone trying to navigate reality. I just qualify it this much to give you a heads-up about my relationship to this happening.

The barnyard used to have two turkeys, Lenard and Jerry. Now these two turkeys were not the sharpest tools in the shed. They, in the course of many conversations, had institutionalized a feud with some of the goats. It was one of those enduring conflicts that everyone involved seemed to feed by their comments and behavior. I asked some of the other barnyard animals about the motive of this ongoing dissension long ago, and they told me, as they remembered it, the two sides simply liked fighting with each other.

It takes a mighty imagination to find conflict when all the beauty and poetry of the world beckons. I guess that's what most of the other animals thought about the ongoing strife between the turkeys and goats. That was at least what they communicated in public. I noticed, however, that these bystanders did enjoy and take pleasure in this conflict. Just as an individual might have a foible, the community carries the same fault in its society.

I only tell you this because it was really a collective phenomenon that unfolded there in the barnyard long ago. It's true that it was driven by the turkeys and goats, but all the individuals I questioned about this episode agreed that the whole community participated in some fashion regarding this whole affair.

Obviously and unfortunately, I cannot re-create the vitriolic nature of these arguments of long ago. Trying to do so would, I'm sure, vitiate the messages long ago traded by these old adversaries. Let me then just attempt to paraphrase the apparent mood that their ongoing fracas created. Indeed it was, I'm told, a most nonsensical disagreement. The things these two groups fought about made the big-enders and small-enders look like sophisticated diplomats.

It then, however, would be a more than fair question for you to ask why then drag these fools back into the light of day. Just this and I'll try to be to the point here. It was because they triggered and aggravated each other with hyperbole. They did this with passion and relentless intent. There were no boundaries to their exaggerations. They lived to get the last word. They ached to have a comment that stilled the small mouth sounds of the other side. We've all been there in truth. It was argument for argument sake, and everyone knew it.

A good historian attempts to re-create the scene so others may look in and see what took place there long ago. With that target in mind, I will then paint a scenario of some of those long ago verbal battles so you can see the landscape and absurdity of these arguments. Why? I hear the crowd roar. We will hopefully then never have to traverse this terrain again, in hopes that seeing this example of sheer stupidity might give us the perfect lesson of what to avoid in the future.

This is how it was told to me. Lenard was going by the goat pen and commented on the hideous smell there.

A number of goats overheard this comment, and they responded, "It doesn't smell as bad as the turkey cage, and we think someone is smelling himself."

You can see right away that this was not debate club material, more in fact like a number of idiots stumbling on a way to embarrass themselves. Jerry got pulled into the strife quite early after that initial salvo of poorly constructed comments directed at the opposing team. Lenard explained to Jerry how these four-legged brutes had insulted him, and his kind. Jerry's response was to run over within hearing distance to the goat pen and hurl disrespectful epithets at the goats. As you might well imagine, this was akin to stirring a bowl of poop.

The goats, who were never known for their sharp intellectual acuity, responded with some of the most basic, low-down, poorly constructed insults that any besieged individuals might construct. They were heard to say such things as, "Your momma likes to walk through manure, and turkeys are dumb."

The last insult there was one they felt particularly fond of repeating, and they actually continue to say it today when someone makes a mistake. They evidently felt like they had hit the motherlode of creativity with that one.

Now what was interesting in this stylized conflict was not so much how the goats handled the situation, but what the two turkeys did with this entire miasma. The goats were always getting into hostilities with other species and, for that matter, with each other. It was almost like they were Irish. The turkeys, however, were not used to this type of disquieting interaction. They started to crack under the pressure.

Truth be told, the internal environment of any individual does best when it focuses on love, communion, and what we all share as a community. I'm not denigrating any species when I say that turkeys are simple creatures. The axis of understanding around which the turkeys existed was really a simple theorem. Love your neighbor, eat your feed, and stay out of the rain. The last one there was because of the thing about looking up in a rainstorm and possibly drowning because of it. It was not a bad theorem and might be used by any species for that matter. Lenard and Jerry had, however, accidently overstepped their natural boundaries. The conflict for them was like quicksand.

They responded in kind to each insult hurled at them, thinking it would end the matter only to find a new affront sitting on their doorstep. I don't suppose there is a universal lesson buried within this story, but if there were, Lenard and Jerry didn't see it. They kept on returning the offensive slurs. It was sad to watch because, with each volley returned, the two turkeys fell deeper into a melancholy depression. They spent the rest of their days saying inarticulately, "Gobble, gobble, gobble."

The Singing 20 Flowers

Rocko has a secret. I heard about this in the strangest way I've ever learned about anything. First I should tell you about Rocko's secret, but it's hard to focus on that without telling you how I heard about all this. Now on top of that, I'm almost afraid to tell you how I came to know it because really I'm fearful that it's quite unbelievable in the normal course of events and also I've sorta been warned.

Decisions, decisions, decisions. Well, okay. Here's what happened. Last weekend I went fishing. There is a good spot down by the old bridge. The water there is quite deep, and usually some rainbow trout are hiding under the logs that hang over the creek there. I was leaning back against the trunk of a tree with my line in the water, just enjoying a lazy day. That's when I heard it.

At first it was general, and there were no distinctive sounds in it. I turned to see where it was coming from. Up away from the bank is a field of lilies just beyond where the creek usually stops flooding in spring. These bell-shaped, white flowers seemed to be moving in unison, and out of the mouth of these many bells, a sound was coming. The improbable surprises you; the impossible astonishes. That was my reaction. I could do nothing but watch and listen as the lilies picked up a stronger cadence to their emerging song.

I was even more flabbergasted as very distinctive sounds like voices started to emerge from these flowers. I could not believe my eyes or ears. At first the voices were not at all distinctive or clear, but as the sound got louder and more rhythmic, I could hear a strange duel of words happening inside the sound. It was like an argument but not against anything but rather against the phenomenon of silence itself.

I know that's hard to understand, but it was like the voices were reacting to each other and busily filling the void of silence there in the meadow next to the creek. I was so amazed at what was happening that I hardly noticed when they, the voices, became coherent and you could begin to understand what was being said. The moment that occurred to me, my jaw dropped open. I could understand the lilies of the valley.

Now it took me a moment to gather my senses enough to not only listen to what was being said but to put it into context. I understood almost immediately that the different voices were from the same source. It was like an argument we might have inside our mind. There was an agility and grace to the argument, a forgiving, challenging energy that pushed through the music. You could not help but be drawn into the deliberation. It was enticing and vexing all at once.

My disbelief deepened as I realized I knew the subject of the song. I will tell you matter of fact who the song was about, but first I really have to tell you that the medium of how I received this information was actually beautiful. It was a sound, and there were words, but the lilies grabbed at a part of me that I didn't even know existed. It was like being spoken to in a strange language via a sense you didn't know you had prior to this experience. I felt like these flowers were seducing me. It was totally mesmerizing except for the content.

It took me a while to focus and then to understand the content of the song. Surprise stacked upon disbelief creates a rather flimsy structure. However, there it was. It was a song about Red the Rooster. While the content of the song existed within this beautifully delicate complex structure, the idea of it was very simple. The song argued about the value of a friendship. It gave point and counterpoint in a dazzling, dizzy dissertation about the qualities necessary for friendship. It was very personal and to the point of the possibility of having this friendship. The voice of the flowers somehow also communicated the emotions involved in this relationship.

My heart became the map upon which this argument took place. It was not difficult, but rather terribly simple to realize that the creator of this song was Rocko the Mean Butterfly. I realized in that moment that I had been sitting in a very twisted, uncomfortable position. The mystery and magic of the event had frozen me into a listening, seeing statue.

I rolled over and stood up. The whole experience was surreal. Slowly I walked up toward the flowers. The song continued its probing insights into the concept of friendships as I reached the flowers. Here among them there was also a vibration from them. Here it was not a seeing, hearing, or feeling but rather a knowing. Even though there was an argument in the song, there was a comfort to the soul. I was about to sit down among the flowers when, all of a sudden, they stuttered to an abrupt end.

The silence after that beautiful music was too much. It felt like I was naked with no place to hide. It's strange to say, but the silence startled me.

Right after that, a challenging voice startled me again, "What are you doing here?"

It was Rocko, and I immediately understood that he was angry. Now here was a tiny animal that I could crush in my hand, but I realized I was terrified. I can't explain why I was so frightened, but every instinct in my body told me to be so. I apologized profusely and explained how I had been fishing and heard the flowers begin to sing and could not help but be drawn into it. I could feel that the moment of lethal danger had passed. Rocko had been sitting up wind of the flowers on some tree branches. The tenor in his voice relaxed. He still looked upset, but he was not apparently going to do anything about it.

"Rocko," I asked, "how is it that the flowers can sing your thoughts?"

"When you're full of pollen, the day is warm, and the wind is right. Butterflies can make almost any plant that's sensitive sing their thoughts," said Rocko. "We often do it like you just heard to know our thoughts better. We also court our ladies and give warnings to our enemies that way. Butterflies have strong relationships with all sorts of plants." Rocko appeared to have another thought, and in a second, he flew up in a menacing way above my head. "Look, you creatures shouldn't know anything about this, and furthermore I don't like you knowing my thoughts about my friendship with Red. It will be to your advantage and safety to not discuss what you saw and heard here today."

In a flash he was gone. This was such an amazing thing that I felt I had to share it with someone. However, please don't tell anyone I told you about this. I'm actually afraid of Rocko the Mean Butterfly. Can we just keep this between us?

Leon the Pigeon

I was over in the barn the other day visiting Mildred the Mare, just really passing time when she asked me to get some hay from the loft for her. I went up into the loft to get the hay when I noticed how many pigeons were there in the barn. They were flying about and sort of captured in their own reality, so to speak. I noticed that one pigeon specifically seemed to be leading the charge.

I stopped and watched them for a brief moment and noticed, when I did so, they almost immediately took notice of my attention. I'm not sure if they realized that I noticed that they noticed me. I only say that because of what happened shortly thereafter. They began to fly in what can only be described as a very busy way. They were just there right above me when I was pelted from above by bird poop.

Now birds, because of their beaks, don't laugh the way other animals do. The flock in unison swept toward the highest arch of the barn and settled onto their roosts. If it were not laughter, it was a good mimic of it. I was insulted and offended. I looked up at them and did take notice that their aforementioned leader seemed to be especially enjoying this humiliation that I had suffered. The flock was definitely aware of my anger, and that seemed to fuel their laughter more.

I have never held a negative attitude toward any species, no matter how malefic their image is in consensual knowledge. I did not want to change my principles based on one incident and especially regarding pigeons because previously I had a rather beneficent attitude toward them. I turned around, and with as much dignity as I could muster with bird poop on my shoulder, I left the hayloft.

I went back to Mildred's stall and asked her about the pigeons, especially the one that appeared to be their leader. It was interesting because Mildred knew immediately whom I was describing. In fact, as I asked about the barnyard, it only took a slight description of this pigeon to elicit confirmation that he was quite well-known to the whole community. It was a bit of a surprise, however, to hear the varied opinions held by members of the barnyard regarding this pigeon.

It turned out that, in general, he was well-liked. There were some outliers regarding this consensus, but generally speaking, most of the farm animals liked this pigeon that I quickly learned was named Leon. He was known to have a friendly affect and good disposition. The other animals reported that he had a forceful personality that was bordering on the commanding. This came as quite a surprise to me after my initial interaction with Leon, so my curiosity was piqued into finding out more about this interesting character.

I did not know how to speak pigeon so I was at a bit of a loss in regards to going to the source. I went and asked Red the Rooster about this language barrier, and he was quite knowledgeable about this area. He told me that their language was not significantly different than chicken speak, but the feral pigeons had a dialect that was quite different and difficult to understand for the domesticated animals. He also added that these feral pigeons like Leon are sometimes referred to as rats with wings. I found this bit of information intriguing.

I told Red what happened in the hayloft, and he sympathized with my hurt feelings. I further explained that I wanted to find out more about Leon before I got hold of him and wrenched his scrawny little neck.

"I wanted to be fair," I said.

Red looked at me with the eyes of a wise, old rooster. "I'm glad you want to find out more about Leon. I think you will be surprised by what you find out, and it just may change your feelings about this rascal."

I was methodical if nothing else. I began to interview all the animals in the barnyard about Leon. I began to learn about a pigeon that did not fit my image created there in the hayloft. It was funny because, the more information I got about Leon, the more complex and dynamic he became in my imagination. I wondered about all this as I was drawn deeper into my research about Leon.

The geese described him as having a somewhat pushy personality, but once you got to know him, they said he was self-deprecating and funny. He made jokes that were funny and held himself up in the self-scrutiny that humor was so good at doing. They said he was playful and energetic and always open to dialogue. The pigs said he was great. They described a fellow that was fun to have around and always open to philosophical discussion.

He would at times stand on their backs and eat the bugs that continuously tormented the pigs. This behavior alone gave Leon high marks among the pigs. They also commented that Leon was very adept at word play, a notable achievement for his species. He did this with his ability to make puns, double entendre, and the like.

The goats were less complimentary but nevertheless described an individual that was congenial and responsive to their social needs. I was surprised that the goats did not denigrate the pigeons in general, so I took this rather neutral assessment as praise from this otherwise critical specie. The swans and ducks were also not quite as effusive but did mention Leon and his commandos (their words not mine) as willing to share feed and being open to peaceful coexistence.

The cows surprised me by saying they enjoyed the company of the pigeons in the pasture because they kept some of the bugs away, and the pigeons' presence gave a certain cadence to the pasture experience that the cows felt was pleasant. Mildred the Mare knew what had happened to me in the hayloft, so I didn't ask her opinion but was surprised when she offered an outlook that contradicted my hayloft experience.

It was all a bit disconcerting because I guess I had really decided to dislike this character when his cronies bombarded me with their BMs. I had sabotaged my own desire for revenge. The more you learn about an enemy, the more he comes into focus as almost just like yourself or at least some close proximity to that. The thing of it was I guess my feelings had been bruised. All the stuff I learned about Leon became a buffer between Leon and that bruise.

The sun was out there was a soft breeze, and I could smell the flowers from the pasture. Maybe it's not good to hold a grudge. These thoughts made my step lighter, and I felt at peace with the world. I was walking up toward the barn when, out of the loft door high on the barn, flew Leon and his buddies. I watched as they swept high over my head and disappeared. I realized too late that I was again the target for their waste. Sometimes you just feel like some guys are just out to get you.

Marlene Trying to Be a Hawk

I went over to the barnyard last Tuesday and was walking around just to see what was happening. I was down next to the chicken coop, and just as I was walking by, Marlene, one of Red's hens, went running across the chicken coop roof and shouted "Geronimo!" And then she jumped off the chicken coop roof and made a dramatic effort to flap her wings and fly. Needless to say, the effort was more promising than what happened in reality.

Marlene ended up as a dust-covered bunch of feathers rolling along the ground after a very small amount of time when she was actually airborne. Now I'm not fluent in chicken speak but can decipher enough of it, so I could tell what the gist of what she was saying after this failed attempt at becoming airborne. She stomped by me as if I didn't exist, saying to herself, "There has to be a way to do this."

Needless to say, my curiosity was inflamed. I couldn't quite figure out exactly what was going on here. I didn't want to stare, so I pretended to move along even as I saw that Marlene was struggling to regain the chicken coop roof. I kept looking back as I moved down through the barnyard. Not totally watching where I was going, I bumped into Onion the Pig.

Onion said with a degree of delight, "I bet you can't figure that one out, huh?"

"I'm stumped," I admitted.

I could see that Onion was dying to tell me what was going on, but he just wanted to drag it out, knowing that holding this information was somewhat akin to having a key to a box that someone wants into.

"Okay," I said. "I really want to know why Marlene is acting like a bumblebee during mating season."

Onion laughed. "It's even stranger than that."

Onion settled back on his hunches and got comfortable, and I could see that I was about to receive the story.

"Well," he began, "about three days ago, Marlene was resting on a roost next to the chicken coop during the afternoon heat and noticed a hawk soaring on the air currents way high up above the barnyard. She became totally hypnotized by the grace and beauty of what this hawk was effortlessly doing. Marlene became, as they say, transfixed. Well, ever since that afternoon, Marlene has become convinced, since the hawk's a bird and she is too, it's just a matter of time, effort, and learning. Then she can also soar on the winds high above the earth."

A loud grunting sound interrupted Onion's story as Marlene hit the ground next to the chicken coop and rolled into a rather inelegant ball of feathers. Undaunted and apparently none the worse for the wear, Marlene got up and was muttering something to herself as she went back toward the chicken coop to try again. We both turned and watched as Marlene went through her ridiculous ritual of impossible learning.

Onion said, "Chickens don't stop scratching just because worms are scarce, or at least that's what they always say. I don't think, however, that perseverance is the key to unlock this particular problem."

"I agree," I said. "And where is Red, and what are his thoughts on this matter?"

"Oh, he tried to talk to Marlene right after she got this idea and started jumping off high places," said Onion.

"What effect did that have on her attempts to mimic the hawk?" I asked.

"Well," said Onion, "Marlene scolded Red for not trying to fly himself and said, with his high standing in the community, he should be able to learn this skill easily and teach it to his hens. Now every time he comes into close proximity to Marlene, she begins to scold him all over again. Red has been roosting on the fence up near the barn, facing away from the chicken coop. At night he returns to the coop but refuses to even look at Marlene so they have sort of navigated their dispute to a stalemate."

Needless to say, this was a very interesting situation, and I was very curious as to how this would be resolved. Now at the time, I did not know that Red was consulting Rocko the Mean Butterfly about this situation. So after listening to Onion's version of the story that day, I left the barnyard with many more question than answers. It did, however, motivate me to return early the next day to the barnyard to see if there were any new developments.

Marlene had moved her flying efforts to the top of a rail fence that was about twenty feet from the chicken coop. It had two advantages. The fence was not as high, and the other hens were no longer complaining about Marlene periodically running across the chicken coop roof, yelling "Geronimo!" I did, however, take notice that Marlene was beginning to look like a chicken fresh out of a tornado. She looked like a hen that had been in a fight with a large wild animal.

She was continuing her efforts to fly, but even now, anyone could see that she was getting the worst of the deal. I was standing there watching as she came running along the top of the rail fence with a halfhearted squawk of "Geronimo!" The result was no different from all her previous efforts. To her credit, however, she regained her feet after tumbling in the dust and proceeded to return to her launching place. I did take notice that the comments she made while passing me were not repeatable in respectable company.

A rather large crowd of animals was watching this masochistic exercise as the morning passed away. As time went on, it became a bit painful to even be an observer to this exercise in maniacal belief. Just after midmorning, Rocko the

Mean Butterfly came by and fluttered over to where Marlene was about to make another run at the impossible. I was not close enough to hear what he said to Marlene, but a number of other animals who were in closer proximity said that he said, "You're going to receive a visitor soon."

Everyone was very curious, and even Marlene appeared to show some relief at the prospect of some new dimension entering this insane scenario. Not long after that announcement, the barnyard experienced a fast-moving shadow over its total length. The hawk circled a few times, allowing the domesticated animals to become aware of its presence. Even with that, however, the barnyard animals became nervous and anxious with this airborne predator in their environment.

He circled and came in for a landing, defining grace and elegance even as he did so. The power and presence of this creature that ruled the heavens was impressive and magical as he walked over to where Marlene had come down off the fence. I don't speak wild hawk, so this part of the conversation was conveyed to me by some of the other chickens present who can understand that dialect because it's quite similar to chicken speak. He told Marlene that the hawks rule the sky along with some other birds. And as it should be, the chickens, ducks, geese, and swans rule the land. Trying to change that is not possible and should be avoided.

He lifted off and was gone in a flash, but the impression left on Marlene was permanent. Things returned to normal after that, but Rocko was heard to tell Red after the hawk left, "Ya gotta give her credit for trying!"

The Goat Who Cried Wolf

I got somewhat excited about relaying this story to you because I was there when it all began. I was there talking to Red the Rooster when this young goat Sylvester came running up to us and reported that a pack of wild dogs was headed our way. With caution being the better part of valor, everyone went on notice to watch out and be careful. We asked Sylvester where he saw these dogs, and he described seeing them down near the stream. He added they looked like they were headed this way.

Now let me state for the record that there had not been a pack of wild dogs in this area for years. This very fact topped Sylvester's story with a copious amount of curiosity, if not to say doubt. The powers-that-be in the barnyard always act, however, with caution and care so a scouting expedition was sent out to verify Sylvester's story. It was not without a degree of skepticism that they reported back not only the absence of any pack of animals, but they found also no sign of any such group moving through the area.

Sylvester was confronted by their findings, and no one could doubt the sincerity of his absolute assurance that he had indeed witnessed such a band of prowling predators. Now one of the interesting things about goats, if I can state it so bluntly, is that they are just too stupid to lie. I think saying this is perhaps politically incorrect but raises further concern in this particular matter. What indeed did this young goat see? The other animals in the barnyard know the powers and limitations of each other, so this left everyone sort of scratching their heads.

This whole matter would probably have just vanished like dust in a strong breeze except for what happened a few days later. Sylvester came rushing into the barnyard, shouting that a herd of elephants was momentarily going to rush through the barnyard and everyone should get out of the way so they would not be trampled by these large pachyderms. This particular warning rang a bit hollow. It was not because anyone did not fear being trampled by a larger animal, but most of the barnyard animals realized there probably were not any elephants in the neighborhood.

This particular announcement by Sylvester did, however, make him the center of a lot of curiosity. Why did he make such declarations? What did he see that triggered him to make such an absurd statement? Red the Rooster was asked to interview Sylvester and see if it was just a case of loony goat.

Red asked the usual questions any good detective would ask, "What did you have for breakfast this morning? What was your mother's maiden name? How long have you been plain crazy?"

As you can well imagine, while this line of questioning aptly defined the muddy waters of Sylvester's mind, it did not give any hints as to why he was making such preposterous divulgements. Red, by his own admission, was stumped. He decided to take counsel with Rocko the Mean Butterfly, as he often did in difficult cases. Red found Rocko down by the stream, arguing with a dragonfly as to what was the best way to fly backward.

Red broke into the conversation because he felt the situation called for utmost haste in resolving this baffling situation regarding Sylvester.

The dragonfly turned on him and announced, "Just because chickens had lost the power of flight was no reason to deny the importance of conversations like Rocko and I are having."

Red stuttered to a stop. He had forgotten that the conversations of wild animals always toyed with the truth. He had to admit that flying backward would show you where you'd been. He apologized and conceded that their conversation had great merit and interest even if one could not fly at all.

Rocko and the dragonfly finished their conversation, and each politely demonstrated his amazing ability to fly backward as a credible punctuation to a lofty conversation. Red watched and waited for the dragonfly to leave, which he did backward, which was just a bit disconcerting because it was the opposite of how everyone else left an area. The dragonfly kept an eye on him until he was out of sight.

Red described the situation regarding Sylvester to Rocko. He told Rocko how he had questioned the young goat to no effect. He explained how he was quite confused as to why this otherwise apparently innocent young animal was telling such fibs and then sticking to them when confronted by their lack of foundation.

Rocko, who always loved a good mystery, dove to the center of the riddle by asking a very pertinent question, "How stupid is this goat?"

Red explained that Sylvester had average intelligence for a goat and could probably get better test results than any earthworms within crawling distance.

"Fair enough," said Rocko. "It sounds like we'll have to do some real detective work to get to the bottom of this enigma."

They planned to follow Sylvester on his rounds of daily activities at a distance without him knowing they were watching. The next day Red and Rocko watched as Sylvester meandered into the meadow and ate grass. It was not obviously a situation of high drama. Our two sleuths stayed hidden and observant and saw nothing until after Sylvester had filled his belly with rich wild grass.

At that point, the young goat lifted his eyes toward heaven and began to watch the clouds overhead. He did this until he saw a cloud form into the shape of a charging wild buffalo. He immediately responded to this apparition by running into the barnyard and warning everyone to get out of the way of the charging buffalo.

Rocko and Red retuned in a relaxed fashion to the barnyard and were met by everyone saying that Sylvester was at it again. They counseled calm and said they finally understood the problem.

Solving it was entirely a whole other matter, however. Rocko and Red put their heads together and came up with the idea of Sylvester wearing a quite heavy cowbell around his neck. This kept his head focused down most of the time, and he stopped finding demons in the clouds.

He did come running into the barnyard a few weeks later, saying that bumblebees were attacking and about to take over the barnyard. Upon further examination, this was just a result of the mating season for bumblebees, where they went a little crazy and would run into anything and anyone. Everyone knows about that except, I guess, young goats.

Other than this, there were no major occurrences of crying wolf from the young goat. Things settled back into the wonderful boredom of the barnyard.

The Talking Plant

I'm excited to tell you this story from the barnyard, but I have to be up front about the qualifiers to this story. I got this information from Rocko the Mean Butterfly, and he told me this story with one strong restriction. I'm not to try to tell you which plant I'm talking about. It's because, if the feeding hands find out about this plant, they'll dig it up and study it, and this plant wouldn't wish that on a cabbage. They just say it that way because they think cabbages are one of the most boring of plants.

I'm sort of getting ahead of myself here, but Rocko was so adamant about what I couldn't tell you that it left a deep impression on me. I've always been careful to follow his directions regarding the barnyard. So let me give you the gist of what he told me, and then I'll describe some of my experiences and what I found out about this phenomenon. A plant in the pasture can talk to the animals. I know this really came as a shock to me.

Now when I say that this plant can talk to the animals, it doesn't have a voice or anything like that, but rather it can direct thoughts to the animals and pick up their thought when they are in close proximity. It's a form of telepathy of some sort. I never knew this was possible with plants so I was a bit skeptical when I first heard about this. Evidently there is some sort of a symbiosis with the various grazing animals, and this particular plant because it likes it when the animals eat the old top leaves off of it because it reinvigorates its potential for growth.

According to Rocko, this process actually is coordinated by the plant itself, who gives the animal eating the plant directions about how much and what to eat. The vehicle of communication is just thought, so I naturally asked why the feeding hands were not aware of all this. Rocko explained by saying, in this plant, the ego is distributed into many leaves so there is no strong center identity in it. The feeding hands have their ego center stage in their consciousness so they have a hard time even hearing anything outside themselves. It all somewhat makes sense if you think in term of different areas of awareness.

This was all very interesting to me, and I was just a bit thrown off my game by the information that there is awareness where I thought there was none before. Rocko said these plants have the ability to communicate with many other species of plants that the animals cannot communicate with. He went on to explain that this particular plant then, in one sense, becomes the gatekeeper for the plant world. Through this channel of communication with the plants, the animals have a deeper and more fundamental understanding of the plant world.

As you can well imagine, I was deeply interested in seeing if I could communicate with this plant. Rocko explained that would not be possible because I would have to be in close proximity to the plant, and since I was from the feeding hands species, I was not to be trusted with the knowledge of which plant sings its song to both the plant and animal world.

Nothing makes information more valuable than a secret. This bit of knowledge changed the way I began to look at the world. I began to look at all the plants in the pasture with a different eye. One of these was looking back at me in a sense, and I did not know which one it was. I walked the pasture and looked at all the plants there with a deeper interest and more respect.

The next day I found Rocko down behind the pigpen on the wildflowers that grow there. I was eager to ask him more questions about this miracle plant.

"Rocko," I began, "where is the seat of intelligence located in this plant? Where is its brain located?"

"Oh," he said, "as far as I can tell, it's between the root and the flower of the plant. The plant's flower is like its face in a way, and the area leading up to the flower and down to its root is the space where it's evolved a unique and different capacity. It's in that area we think that it's developed the unique instrument to communicate with us."

Rocko continued to describe his theory about this plant in general terms. "There were magic mushrooms that could alter consciousness in certain animals. There were all sorts of plants that were good to eat by various animals. It just made sense that at least one species of plant would make the leap into self-aware consciousness so it could check out what was going on in some larger sense. The intriguing thing is what new insights this plant brought to the animal world."

This aroused my curiosity even more. "What kind of insights did it bring to the animal world?"

"Oh," said Rocko, "a whole new way of looking at the phenomenon of life really. The self-preserving instinct felt by animals is a totally different instinct in plants. In plants, death is a built-in need. They look forward to their dissolution as a way to get back to where they know they came from. They have close and intimate relationships with billions of things in the soil. There in the ground, thoughts, ideas, feelings, and emotions flow in the fluid soil like blood in our bodies. They have described this to me like a very big thanksgiving party where everyone knows everyone, but the party never ends until you rise up again out of the earth to salute the sun.

"Their individuality is also different. It exists in each plant while it's doing its thing with the sun but evaporates into a much more fluid thing once they return to the soil. They don't have vision but rather an awareness of what's closely around them."

I've never had any reason to distrust or not believe anything that either Rocko the Mean Butterfly or Red the Rooster have told me. The information about this plant started to strain credulity and my perception of reality. I said as much to Rocko, and he laughed at my faltering belief.

"It's probably difficult for you," said Rocko, "because you cannot put your finger into the gaping hole of reality this creates in your worldview. The world to you is what you can see, feel, and deduce with your logic. It's like the old Irish proverb: 'Seeing's believing, but feeling is God's own truth.' I can't solve that problem for you, but know this. The world still hides many mysteries from us all."

I went for a walk down into the pasture, and I was looking at all the various plants. I know it really didn't work this way, but I started to talk to them.

"Hello," I said. "How are you on this fine summer day?"

I was met by total silence.. It was pervasive and total, and I wondered what else existed out there that I didn't know about. I relaxed back into my old way of seeing things and realized that things don't change just because you want them to. It did give me pause for thought, however, to realize, when you go for a walk in a pasture, there might be someone else there that you aren't aware of.

It's All in the Name

Sometimes when I'm over in the barnyard, the pleasant environment makes me take notice. On Thursday past, that's exactly how I felt. I had been talking to the pigs, and they were explaining how keeping on your feed as a regular practice keeps you not only healthy physically but happy mentally. Donner was the one explaining this idea, and he seemed to have an inordinate amount of passion when it came to talking about food. They called him Donner because of the historical Donner Pass incident where people ended up eating each other because they were stuck in a snowstorm in the Donner Pass. It wasn't because he would eat anyone. It was because he always acted as if he were starving. The name just stuck.

As I was walking away from the pigpen, Donner returned to his trough. I was struck by how the animals would always take time to chat and pass the time of day with me. I walked over to the goat pen and greeted them all with a pleasant hello and smile. In truth there was a halfhearted reply, and whereas I'm not fluent in goat speak, I did understand that I was the object of a negative comment by Can and Anything. Can got his name from always chewing on cans; Anything got his name from eating almost anything.

I ignored the negative comment and asked all present how things were going. Anything, who was then chewing on a paint rag left near the goat pen by the feeding hands, said that life was difficult and tedious. I was really surprised that he used the word "tedious." Goats didn't usually have great range in their vocabulary words. Ignoring that and his poor pronunciation of the word, I asked him what was wrong. I could see that he was a bit taken back by my question, and he simply mumbled something.

Thinking perhaps that I had caught him on an off day, I excused myself and walked on. I went into the barn where it was cooler and the horses were in their stalls relaxing. I greeted them and gave Mildred a carrot I had saved for her. I must admit that Mildred was always one of my favorites, and it was always fun seeing her even though she was a mare of a few words. I loved the smells of the hay, grain, and such in the barn. I lingered there for a while, then bade my farewell, and walked down to the chicken coop, hoping to see Red the Rooster.

I was approaching the coop when I heard a consistent banging. Red the Rooster came around the coop into my line of sight, and I could see that he was frustrated and angry. The banging was on the opposite side of the coop from where I was so I could not tell what was causing the commotion. Red took up a roost on the fallen log behind the coop between the coop and me. I was a little shy to greet him, seeing that he was upset. I could just tell from the way he roosted that things weren't right.

I walked around into his line of vision so I could introduce myself gently into this disquieted environment. I could see, once I got around in front of Red, he was steaming because his eyes were closed and his face was contorted into a grimace. This was a bit more serious than I initially had thought. I coughed and scuffed my shoes on the ground to let him know I was present. Red looked up and took note of me then.

"Hi," I said. "What's up?"

I could see that Red was bursting to relieve his temper by talking about what had happened. I thought myself quite clever by drawing him out this way.

"Marlene," he said, "is convinced there are grubs hidden in the walls of the chicken coop, and she is pecking at the walls of the coop relentlessly. She is actually making holes in the walls by her persistent pecking." Red slumped down on his roost on the log, and I could swear that I saw steam come out of the top of his head.

"Well," I said, "why don't you get an expert in eating all things and let him have a talk with Marlene?"

"Who would that be?" Red asked.

I immediately thought of Anything, who I had just had a conversation with a short time ago. I explained my recent contact with Anything and how I was impressed by his willingness to eat anything and how it might have some input into the present situation. Red looked a bit skeptical, but I could see that Marlene had gotten on his last nerve so he was willing to try anything.

The real surprise came when Red asked me to be the go-between. He asked if I would ask Anything to come and talk to Marlene. Well, needless to say, I was quite flattered to be brought into the barnyard culture in such an important way. I agreed and said I would immediately go and ask Anything if he would come and talk to Marlene.

I hurried away, and as I was going up to the goat pen, I realized that my relationship with Anything and the goats in general was not of the highest quality. I gave myself a pep talk on the way up to the goat pen, all to the point of getting my goat. I thought, *If I can't talk a goat into doing something, I'm not worth my weight in cow poop.*

I approached Anything, who was still chewing on that paint rag, and he looked up with not even a hint of friendship on his face. Just in that moment, my confidence fled me. I stuttered a greeting and clumsily explained to Anything the point of my errand.

To my utter surprise, Anything's face lit up like a Christmas tree. He was delighted to be asked to counsel one of Red's hens. Just then, as I understood the dynamic taking place, I cringed at the prospect of involving myself in a political and social situation that was a bit beyond me. Would I possibly damage my relationship with Red by allowing a goat to hold court near the chicken coop? The die was cast. The thing was done. It would be what it would be. I walked back down to the chicken coop with Anything still chewing on his paint rag.

Anything walked around the chicken coop where Marlene was pecking away at the walls of the building. Anything raised up his head and walked a bit too stiff. I could see that he thought his mission was of the utmost importance. He added a loud, commanding voice to his swagger and demeanor. Marlene looked at him, and was I could see just a bit caught off guard.

Anything essentially said, if there were grubs there, he would know because of the superior quality of the goat nose he possessed. He sniffed the coop and then started to chew on it. Marlene looked at Anything, shook her head, and walked away.

Red looked at me sardonically. "Now this is a brand-new problem."

I left the barnyard, thinking I should mind my own business. Some problems are just too complex.

Gag the Comedian

I was just wandering around in the barnyard, trying to stay out of trouble when I encountered a strange phenomenon. A goose there was doing a stand-up routine and had a number of the barnyard animals as his audience. This intrigued me, so I stopped and started to listen. He was actually quite good. I guess in any group there's always someone who has a sense of humor. He finished a somewhat short routine, and the group wandered away.

I wanted to find out more about this goose so I asked around. His name was Gag, and he got that name not from telling gags but from the fact that often he would laugh so hard at his own jokes that he would end up gagging. His actual given name was Fusball, but no one called him that anymore. Now not withstanding that slight foible of gagging and the discrepancy in his name, he actually had a real knack for telling jokes and entertaining others.

I started to keep my eye out for him, wanting to catch him doing his routine. It was somewhat difficult because, a lot of the time, he was a hit-and-run comedian. I mean that he would let go a joke in a group he was part of and then sort of blend back into the group. I came upon him the other day as he delivered one of his jokes.

"How do you tell the difference between a goose and a swan?" he asked. "The goose is the one who isn't posing."

He didn't gag on that joke, but you could see that it caught a number of his listeners off guard, especially because they were swans.

Now I've always taken note of the fact that geese are short-tempered, easily agitated creatures who will most often give you their opinion about negative things. On this measure of things, Gag was actually quite a pleasant surprise. The thing of it is, you normally wouldn't expect a goose to take on the role of a comedian. He has managed to create a routine with wings flapping and long neck gyrations that keep the other animals laughing. His material is a bit colloquial, but he has, like I've said, a great delivery and good rapport with his audience. Now every chance I get, I always watch as he performs this second oldest of all professions.

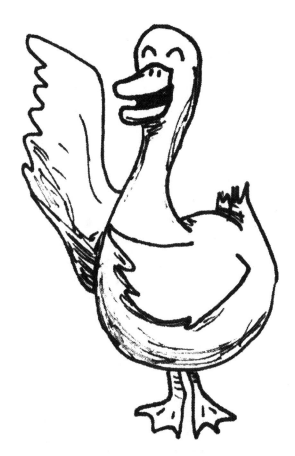

Gag does stand out in a crowd, and I'm not sure if that's because I'm familiar with his reputation or he just does. I saw him at a distance the other day entertaining, so I went over next to the barn where he was holding court.

"A horse, a goat, and a chicken went into a bar. The bartender serves the horse and the goat, but when he comes to the chicken, he cries fowl." He did chuckle a response to that joke.

Now I really must admit to being fascinated by someone's ability to get up and entertain in front of a group. Not only does it seem difficult and dangerous in the sense that you can fail, it also just seems to be a brave thing to do in my mind. Gag wades into a crowd like they belong to him. He seems able to read the tenor and mood of the group and brings them along with his humor until he appears to have total control.

One of the intriguing aspects to Gag's humor is that he plays his height to his advantage. Many of the other animals tower over him as a goose, but I've noticed, on occasion, he creates an amphitheater effect with the height thing. I caught his act the other afternoon when he was surrounded by a number of the stable animals: the goats, the sheep, and the horses. I had to stand on a barrel to see over the crowd.

"How do you tell the difference between a rock and a goat?" asked Gag. "The rock usually knows enough to leave well enough alone."

One of my observations in watching Gag is that he has a certain amount of control over the group in front of him. Now I always wonder how much of that control is given to the comedian by the crowd or how much is taken from them by the comedian. It's really a curious thing to watch because someone like Gag, who is good at it, makes it look effortless and easy. The resonance created by Gag with the audience is sort of like a dance where no one knows what the next step will be. He then delights and surprises with his jokes or antics and carries them ever onward into new territory.

Gag was already doing another setup. "Well, if that didn't work, what would be the second-best way of telling a goat from a rock? Rocks usually don't smell that bad."

It was funny with that last joke because the goats were all laughing until someone pointed out to them that they were being made fun of. They bristled with resentment until someone asked why, and then they realized that their anger had no memory.

A lot of Gag's humor is situational. He actually makes jokes about everyday activities that all the animals engage in.

"How do you tell it's feeding time at the pigpen?" he asked. "It's much like an Irish wake because, even if you're not drunk, acting that way is the best chance for getting more food."

The other day I saw him entertaining some of the ducks, and his lead-in joke was to the point. "What do you call a duck who uses a condom? A safe quacker."

The ducks really seemed to enjoy that joke. Some of the goats were there, and they kept asking the ducks to explain Gag's jokes to them. I swear sometimes with those goats it's like using a wagon in deep snow.

Gag also had the ability to adapt his presentation to who was in his audience. The bull from the neighbor was staying at the barnyard and listening to Gag.

"What's the difference between a wild bull and a domesticated one?" asked Gag. "There is none. That's the problem with that species."

The bull, Gruff, who was actually quite mild mannered, just shook his head and wandered off. Making fun of Gruff was like rain against the side of the barn.

He saw me in the audience and asked, "What's another name for a dumbwaiter?" His reply was, of course, a feeding hands creature.

"Why do they call them feeding hands? Because that's the only part that works," Gag answered.

His ability to tailor his jokes to the audience was creative and quick. I also took note that the jokes were also a balance between funny and insulting to the intended target.

I thought I would sit down with Gag to interview him. He did have the potential for celebrity status at least in the barnyard. He was a bit reluctant at first but then agreed. I won't bother you with the actual conversation. Suffice it to say, Gag was a totally different animal in a one-on-one exchange. He was thoughtful, clever, and insightful. He personified a creature who saw behind the curtain. It made me wonder about what the real building blocks of humor are.

He did say there at the last, "It's not me who is funny but rather the universe."

The Water Hole

Life in the barnyard has a consistency about it. You can always see that something is going on. It is a place where boredom doesn't really exist. There is always something happening. Now the interesting thing about that is the happening things are always just normal stuff like animals interacting, eating, or just grazing. The real excitement takes place in the fact that a lot of the animals are just being there. Yep, doing nothing. They are, however, watching with the patience of dirt itself.

On a day as just described, Red walked down to the water hole. Now you have to understand something about the water hole. It is true that it is where the animals go to drink. It is, however, something more than that. Water, you see, makes life possible. Now I'm not claiming any symbolic or metaphysical quality to the water hole. I mean not really but almost.

All the animals come to the water hole. It's a meeting place. The necessity to quench their thirst makes the water hole hopefully a place of peace. The very fact that it's a meeting place where many animals intermingle also makes it a place where many types of interactions take place. Now not only do all the animals know all this about the watering hole, they go there with that very mental baggage. It's somewhat like being called up on stage and being recognized because you are. The water hole is that and more for the animals of the barnyard.

Now I only describe all that to give you a feel for what was in Red's mind as he walked down to the water hole. Red never liked to drink where the large animals like the horses and cows drank because they trampled the dirt near the edge and turned it into mud. He preferred to walk out on a fallen log that lay protruding into the water a few feet. The water was clear, and from that vantage point, he could watch the other animals as they approached the water and drank.

Red surveyed his domain. He knew he shared it with all the other animals, but the superiority of chickens in his mind was as certain as the sun coming up each day. Red had an abundance of love and caring for all the other animals unless they behaved badly. He watched with fascination as the various animals came down to the water hole and drank. There was a certain beauty to the fact that it all took place in a certain cadence. Everyone took his or her turn and showed respect for those coming both before and after.

A good neighbor in the barnyard was someone who basically ignored you but was there when you needed them. Within the experience of seeing each other was the saying hello. You didn't need to make any noise. It was all very Zen-like. All the animals knew who was there and why—all except the goats sometimes. Not to say anything negative about the goats, I mean they played their part well. It was just that sometimes they were self-absorbed, lazy, selfish, and sometimes stupid. Other than that, they were fine.

A young male goat caused the disturbance. In truth it was not even much of a disturbance initially. It didn't break the inward calm of Red's serenity as he sat on the log. He did, however, watch and observe. The young goat had gone too far into the water, and its front legs had become stuck in the mud there. It brayed its complaint and thrashed about, trying to free itself from the mud. Finally by falling forward and turning, it managed to free itself, scramble up the bank, and bray its complaint against the world. Red watched and observed that the young goat was not only covered in mud but also seemed deeply embarrassed about what had happened to it.

Red could see that there was anger and hostility in the young goat's body. The problem was that there was no one to blame for his predicament. Just then, a large, lumbering cow came down to the water hole to drink. She passed quite closely to the goat and, just by proximity, made the goat move because of the cow's large size. A little, tiny mental mechanism of attack was triggered in the young goat. The little goat stamped his feet, lowered his head, and charged into the belly of the large cow.

The cow flinched just a bit but then turned his backside to the goat and kicked. The poor little goat went tumbling head over heels into a ball on the side of the bank. Red could see that the cow's response caught him totally off guard. All the animals present watched as the goat disentangled himself from the results of the kick. In truth everyone hoped he was not hurt. There was that silent vibration of relaxation as the young goat got up and walked about. He didn't appear to be injured from this rather rough interaction with the cow.

Now here's the thing. In the barnyard, there was no good or bad to what had just happened. It was all just the flow of activity that caused one event to follow the next. Things happen, as they say, and this was a saying from the feeding hands' book of sayings. The watering hole's silence took traction again. The animals all returned to being good neighbors again. Everyone knew the cow meant no harm. It's just a fact of nature that the large animals, by their reactions, can sometimes have derogatory effects upon the smaller animals. In truth it's an acceptable part of barnyard lore for the smaller to get out of the way of the larger.

Now Red had witnessed this disruption to the peace and serenity of the watering hole. He had also taken note of its resolution and the return of that serenity. He also understood that most animals were not as intelligent, observant, and sensitive as chickens. With these thoughts careening through his mind, he realized he had just witnessed the solution of a much larger problem.

Red wrote a letter to the newspaper the next day. He explained how we should all allow each other our space, foibles, and mistakes. He went on to describe how we shouldn't intervene in conflict unless asked or compelled by our own morality. In addition, he said we should even suffer fools and help them when they get into trouble, but we should also allow them to make their mistakes.

Nothing ever came of it. Things returned to normal at the watering hole. Red, on his log, continued to be the witness. He thought, *Maybe it's impossible to describe certain things. Maybe certain places have their own magic and cannot be copied or duplicated.*

Sitting there on the log, Red realized he liked being at the water hole.

A Walk in the Woods

I was out for a walk and really wasn't going anywhere in particular. It was one of those days where the wind and sun combine to make you feel comfortable about the woods around you. I actually felt very content, and maybe that's why I noticed it. A slight disturbance in the breeze played across my face and teased my senses with something unknown.

It drew me deeper into a perspective, and I felt like the world was a mysterious, playful, and enchanting place. At first there were no thoughts along with all of this. It was like a time-out for thinking, and all the magic of the universe wanted to tickle me a bit. I do remember referencing a note to myself that this was nice-nice. I mean, I guess that nice piled on top of more nice takes you to an infrequently visited place.

I must confess to wallowing in this mood and diving deeply into the indulgence it represented. I continued to welcome what was happening to my senses until I noticed a stutter to the whole thing. I don't know how to explain this other than to say this wonderful feeling began to have an internal stutter.

If you're listening to the best orchestra in the world and one of the players is off-key, you hear that and not the best orchestra in the world. That was how this stutter affected me in that moment. The discordance of the stutter brought me back to real-time reality. It was sort of like coming out of warm water into a cool breeze, the charm of where I had been made normal reality unpleasant. I shivered and tried to adjust back to normal.

At that point I noticed that the stutter was actually a form of laughter. Now that I was back into my normal awareness, I saw Rocko the Mean Butterfly sitting on a branch up high in a nearby tree.

I immediately became fearful and suspicious. "Was that you who created those feelings I just had?"

"No!" he said. "I just created a minor wind turbine to channel your feelings into a pleasant place. You were the driver inside the tunnel of wind, and I began to laugh at what you did with it all."

I had a strange mix of emotions with that explanation. Whereas I felt angry because I had been made fun of, I also felt like I was right on the cusp of learning something important about myself. This butterfly really irritated me.

"Why did you laugh at me?" I asked.

I could see that my question changed Rocko's posture. All at once it seemed to me that he began to take the conversation seriously. "I laughed because you began to be greedy about the feelings that were being created."

"I was not," I blurted out. "I was just enjoying them."

"I'm just a butterfly, but I could see," said Rocko, "that the feelings you were having were making you weaker and less focused. They should have made you stronger and more lucid."

It really makes me angry in an argument when the other side is right. I felt like punching Rocko, but first and foremost, he was way up in a tree away from me. And second, I really couldn't envision punching a butterfly. I really wanted this conversation to be over but also wanted to know how to do what Rocko was describing.

"Well, it was very nice seeing you," I said. "Good-bye."

I turned and started to walk away. I thought, *That butterfly has been perfectly named. He is mean and stupid too.* I started to walk faster for a while, and it seemed to make me feel better. The more distance I got between that stupid butterfly and me, the better I thought. My mind kept going back to the meeting and everything Rocko had said, and the more I thought about it, the more upset I became.

"Did you want to ask me a question?" Rocko was on a branch above and ahead of me.

"No!" I said. "I just want to be left alone."

"Oh, okay then. I'll see you around," said Rocko.

He lifted off and started to flutter away. I watched as he flew away, and the silence around me closed in and made me feel very lonely.

"Wait!" I yelled after Rocko as he was gathering distance between us.

Butterflies actually fly very fast, and I watched as he disappeared into the woods behind me. I sat down on a log and felt lonely and sad. *Maybe I should have been better at listening,* I thought. *He didn't have the right to put me into that stupid vortex of wind or whatever he called it.*

On top of that, my feelings are my business, and he could just keep his stupid opinions about stuff like that to himself. I started to see that Rocko was just a no-good busybody who butted into other people's business where he wasn't invited. Why, the next time I see him, I'm gonna give him a piece of my mind and tell him to mind his own business.

"I heard you yell 'Wait!' before." Rocko was back and sitting on a limb not ten feet from me. "I thought I'd give you some private time to think things over."

"Gee, I'm really glad to see you Rocko," I said. "I wanted to ask you a question about our previous conversation."

I thought, *Gee, this character is stealth itself. I don't even know how long he's been sitting there on the limb above me.*

"What is your question?" asked Rocko.

"Well, you said in our earlier conversation that those feelings I had could make me stronger and more aware. How do you do that?" I asked.

"Well," said Rocko, "it's always good to start from where you are at. You initially began to harvest those feelings like they were possessions that you could store and save. Understand first and foremost that it doesn't work that way. You can't keep the magic of a moment to savor it later. You'll have a different moment then with different magic for that new moment.

"Understand also that the universe often offers creativity, power, and insights. Connect them to yourself, and do something with them. I apologize for creating the wind turbine around you. It was very rude to not tell you ahead of time."

"Oh no," I said. "I actually enjoyed the experience very much."

"Butterflies often do that to each other," said Rocko, "and it is a form of play we engage in among us."

I walked back home, thinking that maybe I had learned something and Rocko was not such a bad guy after all.

That was the story of what happened to me on a walk one afternoon. You never know what will happen or what you'll learn when you have friends like Rocko the Mean Butterfly. Sometimes I still think he's a jerk, but I'd never say that to his face.

Goat Story

I just wanted to let you know about this strange event that occurred down at the henhouse in the barnyard. This would not even have come to light except it was a bit funny and a lot of folks (including some animals in the barnyard) had some fun at Red's expense. It was a warm spring day, and all was going well in the barnyard. Red had been surveying his domain and had just congratulated himself on maintaining an organized, well-run clutch of hens. That was until he noticed that Josephine, one of his favorite hens, was chewing on the corner of the chicken coop.

Red usually investigated all aspects of his hens' behaviors. This needed his attention immediately. He went over to where Josephine appeared to be chewing on the coop. He did not want to be overbearing in his approach so he stood in silence and watched as Josephine appeared to be attempting to eat the chicken coop.

"Ahem," he coughed.

Josephine looked up, and he could tell from the look on her face that it was his turn to talk.

"What are you doing?"

"I'm chewing on the chicken coop."

Red was taken back but kept calmness in his voice. "Why are you chewing on the chicken coop?"

"Because that's what goats do," replied Josephine.

To tell the truth, there was a slight increase in Red's voice level as he responded, but there was also still some control. "Josephine, you are a chicken, not a goat."

"I beg to differ," said Josephine. "I'm a goat."

Red in one version was just a rooster in a barnyard with a clutch of hens. The other version was that Red took his job very seriously. He was a manager who attended to all the needs and requirements of his hens. He had a hen who thought she was a goat. This was a serious crisis. He wandered off to his usual roost next to the front of the coop because he wanted to think about this. It also gave him the opportunity to continue to watch Josephine's behavior from a distance. His mind was racing, *Why in the hell did one of his hens think she was one of those four-legged, smelly, garbage disposal systems?*

Red was not prejudiced, but he did take note that the goat was a four-legged beast with no pretty wings like his species. Red rather prided his kind as being similar to the feeding hands creature who was also two-legged like him but lacked the pretty wings that obviously made his kind the most important animal in the barnyard. Why, as proof, didn't the feeding hands come and trade eggs for food every day? He came here; we didn't go there. Who was beholding here? Ha.

Anyway, focus, thought Red. *I have to figure out why Josephine thinks she's a goat and not a chicken. Will this impact her egg-laying skills? Is she going to get along with the other hens, and will they accept a goat living in their midst?*

These and many other thoughts raced through Red's mind as he sat there watching Josephine. He did see early the next day that Josephine wandered over to the goat pen and passively participated in their early morning discussions about the glories of being goats. The goats pretty much ignored her and went about their own business of being goats. Josephine, for her part, still continued to act out the behaviors of a goat. What has affected her behavior?. Why a goat?

Now you might ask, "What's the difference between goat and chicken behavior?"

It's really quite a bit when you get right down to the incidentals. Goats will eat damn near anything. What chickens can eat is measured by the size of their beaks. Chickens are usually quite aware of their surroundings. Goats don't have the same attention span and seem to be able to fall asleep standing up.

But the whole thing of declaring yourself a goat just didn't sit right with Red. In truth it seemed just a tad unpatriotic or something to that affect. Now this probably doesn't sound important to someone who isn't holding the pride of chickendom in their hands, but for someone like Red who was, this was a crisis without borders.

Days passed, and Josephine persisted in her erratic and illogical behavior. She would climb up on things and act like she was chewing her cud, like goats do. She would chew on all sorts of garbage and attempt to eat stuff that a chicken ought not to do. But the worst of it was she would attempt to baaa like a goat, and a chicken attempting to make goat sounds just really didn't work well. It sounded like some animal caught in the cogs of a machine. She always drew attention to herself making these noises, and Red noticed some of the other hens just shaking their heads when they heard Josephine's goat sounds.

Red would take counsel with almost anyone when he had a serious problem, but for a problem of this mystifying quality, he really wanted to touch base with Rocko the Mean Butterfly. He got his opportunity a few days later when he saw Rocko landing on some of the flowers in the barnyard.

He hastened over to where Rocko was scarfing up some nectar and engaged him with a polite greeting. Red explained the situation and behaviors of Josephine and asked Rocko what he thought of the whole matter. Rocko always thought that those hens of Red's were not candidates for a brain trust, but he knew enough not to say that to Red. After a moment's thought, Rocko leaned over and whispered something into Red's ears. He then laughed and flew away.

Red, with a quizzical look on his face, asked himself aloud, "Could that work?"

The next day Red went over to Josephine, jumped up, and stood on her back. He just stood there.

Josephine said, "Excuse me. What are you doing?"

Red said, "Well, since you're a goat a lot of the time, chickens often roost on top of goats' backs in the barnyard."

"Oh," said Josephine, "that's true, but I don't like it."

"Well," said Red, "you have to take the good with the bad."

Red maintained his tenuous roost until he felt it was really tiring Josephine out. Every day after that, Red made it a point to roost for some time right on top of Josephine's back.

A little while after he continued this behavior, the hens were all returning to the coop in the evening one night when Red asked Josephine how it was going being a goat.

Josephine looked up at Red. "I don't want to be a goat anymore. I want to be a chicken."

The feeling of warmth, happiness, and success flooded Red's heart. He didn't say anything about his efforts. He just nodded. "Glad to have you back again, Josephine."

He watched in the following days and monitored very closely to see that Josephine's behaviors were all chicken behaviors. He also noted with pride, even throughout all of this, Josephine never floundered in her egg-laying capacity. She remained one of the best egg producers in the coop despite her dalliance with being a goat.

A few days later, Rocko was flying over the barnyard when Red was reinforcing Josephine's chicken behaviors. As he was flying away, he heard Red exclaim to Josephine why she was such a good chicken.

Rocko thought, *Just as I thought, you have to tell those dumb clucks that they are chickens. No danger of a brain trust there.* He then laughed.

Chasing Pleasure

You know I'm not a gossip. Now that being said, I must admit, when I overhear an interesting story, I can't help but relay it for the possible benefit buried within it. Now I hope I've captured the gist of this exchange, and I say that because I felt like there were some subtle innuendoes involved in this discourse that spoke to the observer within us all.

Rocko had hit every flower around the barnyard and was taking a break on top of the barn. He was sitting there watching the animals in a sort of lazy, half-mindful way. It was really time for a nap, but then he noticed something that stirred his curiosity. Denise, one of Red's hens, was continually running from here to there and back again. Well, that's not very accurate. Every minute or so as time passed, Rocko would see her run across the barnyard to another part of the barnyard.

It was sporadic but consistent. Every few minutes and sometimes longer, Denise could be seen hurrying to some other place than where she had been. Rocko knew Denise was not the sharpest tool in the shed, but still he was curious as to what was the cause of this behavior. He observed that she was not scared or fearful in her movements but rather seemed excited and delighted to be hurrying here and there.

Denise had come to Rocko's attention a long time ago when someone referred to her as a social butterfly in his presence. At the time, this reference to butterfly qualities in someone like Denise had truly baffled Rocko. He never did understand the comparison but had let it go, knowing that other animals were not as intelligent, logical, and precise as butterflies.. Actually this previous association and comparison had tuned Rocko in to observing Denise just a bit more closely. Butterfly are, by nature, very curious and lifelong learners. Rocko was forever trying to figure out which social activities of Denise were at all butterfly like.

Rocko watched and observed that Denise would spend some time with one group of hens, and once that conversation seemed to be fading, she would run across the yard and join another hen group. It was, however, not only the social groupings that attracted her but also any point where food became an issue. If the pigs were being fed, Denise ran over and vicariously took part in the celebration that food always caused in the barnyard. Also any type of interchange among animals that caused a gathering or commotion attracted her attention, and she was right there. If the barnyard had needed a communication specialist, Denise was the lady for the job.

Rocko watched until he became totally perplexed. He reminded himself at that point to ask Red the Rooster about Denise's behavior. Now that opportunity presented itself in a New York minute. Red had been making the rounds, seeing to his hens and their comfort. Satisfied that all was as it should be, Red took up a roost on the horse fence next to the barn. Rocko took the opportunity to flutter down and situated himself on one of the posts of that fence.

Cordial greetings accomplished, Rocko waded into the question uppermost in his mind by describing Denise's behavior and wondering as to its cause.

Red laughed. "Oh, that's Denise. She runs after any possibility of pleasure. Now she thinks that it's always happening where she's not. The thing of it is, she always thinks happiness or pleasure is somehow bubbling to the surface in a group or where any activity gathers attention. She's always been that way, and in her scramble for pleasure, she's met every animal, both wild and domesticated, within hailing distance."

"What a silly ninny," said Rocko as he put together his observations with Red's description.

"Oh no. Not really," said Red. "Her attempt to capture the ghost of what we all want sometimes actually creates it out of thin air."

"What do you mean?" asked Rocko.

"Well," said Red, "Denise is superficial and silly, and that's obvious to anyone who deals with her for any length of time. However, she comes with an open heart, and that somehow injects something invisible into most groups she goes blundering into."

"Well," said Rocko, "that sounds more like she's an annoyance than anything."

"She can be," said Red. "And more than once, I've heard her described as a car alarm that won't shut off. But here's the thing. Denise really reminds everyone she comes in contact with that desire fires the will to live. The greatest causality in everyday living is when that desire somehow gets damaged by the daily grind of life. Denise is the antidote to that, whether we want it or not."

"Yeah," said Rocko, smiling.

"The thing is," said Red, "all creatures treat each other very badly. So here comes someone who sees the other as a source of pleasure. I just think we should get out of her way just a bit and see if she maybe won't create a new playing field."

Rocko laughed. "I guess there's no harm in that."

Just then, they watched as Denise went running after a group of hens that were strolling over in a group to get a drink of water. Both Red and Rocko stopped their exchange as they eavesdropped on the conversation of the group that Denise now came barging into.

"Hi, girls," said Denise. "Where are you gals going?"

Ruth, the lead hen present, explained they were going to go over and all get a drink of water.

"Oh, great," said Denise. "Can I come?"

"Sure," said Ruth. "How are things going with you, Denise?" The conversation faded out as the distance increased between Red, Rocko, and the hens.

Red turned to Rocko. "There is something buried inside the smallest exchanges. It's a promise of a contract that goes way beyond anyone's conscious knowing. Civil communication holds within it the structural foundation of our basic identity. When that is traded among creatures, our identities get reified and confirmed. Doing that reassures us on some fundamental level that society works. Without it, it doesn't. So it seems that Denise has brought to the surface the strongest glue of all, love."

Rocko flew away, thinking, *Those chickens aren't so stupid after all.*

A Love Song

I was over in the barnyard the other day and had an interesting experience. I guess it was mostly the effect it had upon me, but the whole thing started with these two simple songbirds singing. Rocko the Mean Butterfly, and Red the Rooster, and I were sitting under the oak tree just up from the barn. It was a warm, sunny day with a slight breeze, and all was right with the world. We had been talking about the barnyard community and how everyone looked after each other there.

The conversation had wound down, and the sounds of the barnyard drifted into the larger silence between us. It was somewhat comforting to be there with old friends and the familiar noises. I could tell that both Red and Rocko were enjoying the moment because they were relaxed and the need to communicate took second place to just being there with friends. That's when it happened, this strangest of all things.

While we were sitting there, these two tiny songbirds landed on one of the lower branches of the oak tree and began to sing. Now it seemed to me that this simple birdsong came through from thousands of years of practice from this species. I can't even begin to describe the effect that this simple song had upon me. It captured my soul and held it in a loving embrace. It sounds silly to describe the overwhelming potency that this song had upon me. Let me, however, nibble at the edges of this wonderful memory.

The sound was delicate and tiny, yet it reminded me of a vast cathedral filled with Gregorian chant. I can't say why this tiny sound spoke to me of the power and force of love. It was there in a strange, naked beauty that began to disclose the hidden fabric of the universe normally just out of our reach. It was like these two small creatures created an implausible wormhole of sound that allowed something wonderful to come into our world.

It allowed me to see that we are magical creatures. Our real identity is in our present moment awareness. The ego is just a pauper holding its own lie. All the problems and pain in life began to melt away. There was just no one there to carry on that sad tradition. The me was gone, replaced by a living awareness that was animated and vibrant. No longer tied to the wrack of time, I was in resonance with something deep inside of reality.

It's said that the real glue that holds the universe together is music. As I was listening to these two little creatures, that was confirmed. Their song said that we all are one. The meaning inside the song vibrated that the strongest connection among us all is a deep caring. It spoke to the fact that all living creatures deserve consideration and attention. It was beyond comprehension, but this sweet, little song said the dimension holding all of us is made of consciousness and is alive.

I stopped and looked around, thinking maybe I was dreaming. I looked up, and the two birds continued to sing. They pulled me deeper into a vortex of reverential reality. I could not resist. It was like a force of nature. It resonated with something deep inside of what I am. It was seduction from the inside. It said I am the creator. The shape, form, and meaning of the universe is my doing. It was not a pompous, loud motion, but rather something that's always been inside of what I am.

It said I've always been creating, and now seeing this clearly, I saw I could be free from all my fears and negative thoughts. I did not have to forgive anyone but myself. The historical model began to melt, and the song said not to indulge the person I think I am. Lifted beyond the normal caring, I saw that we all are connected. It is not an object connection but rather a deeper association that cannot be broken. While the song created the vehicle, I also saw that my seeing gave me power and tremendous insight.

Swept along in this magical moment, I saw the connection among us all is unbreakable. There is no logic either up or down that can change that. It is not a matter of ideology or belief. The fabric from which we are all made is the same. Thousands of words to page can't change that. The reassurance of that had a profound effect upon my body. I relaxed because all my fears had fled. Nothing in the universe could ever hurt me.

Drawn into a deeper enchantment, I realized the music was inside of me. Tiny though, the sound of the birdsong was it contained the universe.

Magical, hypnotic, and stunned, I saw that reality was my slave. Tipping the world on end like that, I fell through to a greater freedom. I felt a great wave of tumultuous energy all around me even as I sensed a deep, quiet, still peace at my core.

There were no directions anywhere now, but I sensed a great energy foaming toward me. Massive, powerful, and unstoppable, it rolled relentlessly toward me. Its vibration resonated with something inside of me. I was not afraid as it washed over me like a gigantic tsunami, and I realized it was the universe laughing. The sheer makeup of this wave was so unique and powerful that it rattled my physical body. While all of this was happening, I still felt the quiet, serene center inside of me.

This experience sounds like it carried me far afield, but in truth it was just the opposite. I felt like I was coming home for one of the first times. I looked around and saw the familiar and the known. The rocks, trees, and very dirt greeted me with an intimacy that pulled me closer to everything I know. Red and Rocko both smiled at me as if acknowledging a common synonymy.

The birds sang on, weaving the world into a tighter knit. How could it be that so much meaning could be crammed into a tiny birdsong? Some of the other animals had gathered, attracted by the song. There was a quiet, polite, reverent listening. I suspected these tiny creatures spoke to all in various tongues. The two songbirds completed their impromptu musicale.

The barnyard in an instant felt frozen by silence, deep and unending. All present fell into it with no protection. The contrast with the music gone was shocking, and it held us for some seconds, unable to reorient ourselves. Someone coughed, and it shattered the shell of memory and the lost song. Slowly the group regained its social boundaries. Awake from what felt like a dream, I could sense that those present wanted to talk about their experience.

George, one of the pigs present, exclaimed that he was very glad for the existence of songbirds.

Rocko spoke up, "The barnyard deserved such a rousing performance, and I was delighted to be present when it happened."

Gary, one of the goats that had come in rather late to the performance, said, "They really are pesky, noisy creatures, aren't they?"

I guess it is the consumer after all who has the last say.

Bowser

Just knowing Red the Rooster and Rocko the Mean Butterfly, I'm used to creative solutions to problems, but this last go-round in the barnyard really made me laugh. The feeding hands keep two dogs that usually stay up at the house and don't venture into the barnyard. Well, they do come down to the barnyard sometimes with the feeding hands at feeding time, but usually they come and go without incident.

Bowser, a large German shepherd, broke that tradition by coming down to the barnyard by himself. At first he just strolled around and looked things over until he came down next to the chicken coop. He saw some of the hens scratching for food, and he went into this crouching pose where he gathered close to the ground and slinked forward. The hens saw him and became rattled, and they set off the alarm, and all took cover in the coop.

Red had heard the hens' alarm and had come running. He brandished a brazen flashing of wings while crowing loudly. Bowser didn't quite know what to do with all that, and after acting somewhat embarrassed, he shyly ran back to his doghouse up near the big house.

Now Red was not particularly worried or threatened by Bowser, but he was a bit irritated that this dog was disrupting his tranquil days in the barnyard. That irritation led him to disgorge some bile about Bowser when he happened to run into Rocko the Mean Butterfly the next day. Rocko was surprised by Red's irritation because usually Red had a rather peaceful demeanor and attitude about the other animals he lived around.

It had not dawned on Red to ask Rocko for help in this matter, but with Rocko right there, he inquired, "What would you do to get rid of this irritation?"

Rocko thought for a moment. "You know it's more complicated than some predator coming into the barnyard and threatening your hens. The dogs are technically a part of the animals here in the barnyard."

Rocko then asked Red to tell him everything he knew about the dogs.

Red thought for a moment. "Well, not much. I do hear them barking on occasions when a stranger comes into the yard or close to the house. They also communicate sometimes with other dogs far away by long periods of barking either early in the morning or late at night."

"What do they communicate in those exchanges?" asked Rocko.

"Well," said Red, "I'm not fluent in the dog language but do understand enough of it to tell you it's a very silly conversation."

"How so?" asked Rocko.

"Well," said Red, "first the dogs here at the farm bark their message that they are very stupid, and then the dogs farther away reply with the message that they hear them and agree. This can go on for quite some time with each side competing for the title of being the dumbest."

"Very interesting," said Rocko. "It appears that their close association with the feeding hands seems to have damaged their intelligence severely. This antisocial behavior is probably a rebellion against their slavery and an attempt to regain their pre-domestication condition. Living close and under the supervision of the feeding hands must be a very confusing situation for these animals."

"I see," said Red, "but it still doesn't solve my problem. I've got this confused domesticated predator thinking he'd like to make a meal of one of my hens."

"And," said Rocko, "the fact that he's one of the animals here on the farm makes him a double threat because you never know when he'll decide to wander down to the chicken coop and act out his forgotten wild memories on one of your hens. Let me think on this. An animal controlled by the feeding hands should be no problem to control for a butterfly. I'll come by tomorrow." He lifted off and fluttered away for the evening.

Early the next day, as Red emerged from the chicken coop in the morning, Rocko was there. "I think I know how to solve your problem and take away the task of having to keep an eye on Bowser constantly."

"Oh, great," said Red. "What should I do?"

"The first thing," said Rocko, "is you need to have a conversation with the geese."

"Oh, gee," said Red. "That's a task in and of itself. They think they're the center of the universe."

"Precisely," said Rocko. "They will do nothing to help you, but if they think the dog in the barnyard is affecting them, they will take care of business pronto. Just tell them, when a dog chases a chicken, he starts to bark in the barnyard. And once that happens, it causes cracks in the geese eggs."

Early in the afternoon, Red sauntered over to where the geese were hobnobbing. They always tolerated Red's presence and, on occasion, enjoyed his conversations. They thought he had probably been a goose in a previous life. Red, a diplomat to the core, opened his conversation by complimenting the geese on their command of the barnyard.

Red explained the situation and his concerns about how barking dogs could have an effect on chicken eggs, and he was also concerned that this might also be true of goose eggs. He could see immediately that this concern spread like a virus through the geese. Now it's relatively well known in the barnyard that geese are sort of dogmatic in their beliefs. It's just that, once they get an idea, they sort of run with it.

A few days later, Bowser came stealing into the barnyard. The poor dear didn't even get a chance to bark. Those geese hit him like a bunch of kamikaze commandos. They put their long necks close to the ground as they ran up to that poor dog and nipped him in the hind quarters. The thing was they charged him from every side as he tried to walk through the barnyard. He was like a spot of oil on a hot plate. In less than a minute, he was hightailing it back to the big house with his tail between his legs and a loud whimpering coming from that barking machine.

Bowser did return to the barnyard, but only in the presence of the feeding hands. He looked very nervous, and every time he heard a goose honk, he let out a whelp, sounding like a puppy more than the full-grown dog he was. Red and Rocko had a good laugh over the whole affair, agreeing that it was good not to get your hands dirty.

Things returned to normal, and Rocko never bothered to charge a consulting fee. It was just the way of the barnyard.

Circus to Town 33

I was hanging out over at the barnyard, and Rocko the Mean Butterfly and Red the Rooster were talking. Rocko told this story about his grandfather. This happened years ago, but still I thought it was an interesting story to pass along. Every year long ago, the circus used to come to town. On one of these visits, their lion got loose from the circus.

It was quite the scare throughout the community, and everyone was warned to stay indoors until this lion could be located and captured. The barnyard animals were less concerned, I guess, because they seemed to think that she was one of them. Anyway it turned out that this lion had quite an appetite for domesticated animals. The goats bore the brunt of her initial attacks, and it didn't take long for all the other animals as well as the goats to start to guard against becoming her next meal.

The fear this created in the barnyard and the community in general was pervasive. The animals stayed in their barns, stalls, and coops. Everyone was looking over their shoulders as it were and became very nervous and concerned. It came to the point that everyone going outside wanted to go with someone they could outrun. They realized that being with someone slower than themselves meant they could survive to the next day. In reality it was a terrible way to view your neighbor.

The goats took the lead in becoming her meals because they thought they could talk the lion out of wanting to eat them. It was the one time everyone wanted to hang out with the goats. They sort of became the lightning rod for these attacks. It appeared that, even when they were not trying to talk the lion out of attacking and eating them, they were not very quick at getting out of the way of the attack once it was launched. The other aspect to attacking the goats was that they didn't stick up for one another.

The lion attacked a goose once, and all the other geese went into attack mode. While the lion held the poor goose unfortunate enough to be singled out, the other geese attacked. They came at the lion from every angle and with a relentlessness that was awesome. The lion tried to respond to their persistent nips and bites, but there were so many of them that, in the mayhem, she lost her hold on the initial victim. That goose escaped with some serious injuries but at least lived to tell the tale.

As time went on, even the goats began to catch on and became a bit more cunning at avoiding becoming the lion's next morsel. The lion took up residence in the woods next to the farm and started to become much more patient in waiting for his next meal. The initial introduction of the lion into the area around the barnyard had been a giveaway to this predator in terms of him getting something to eat. The local animals, both wild and domesticated, were simply not used to such rapacious behavior.

At the point when the lion was living in the woods next to the farm, Rocko's grandfather was asked to intercede in the matter. Rupert, Rocko's grandfather, was an old school guy who had forgotten more stuff than most guys know.

He asked, "What do you want me to do?"

"Well," they said, "it would be great if you could capture the lion, but we know you can't probably do that so can you just scare him away."

Rupert laughed at that and, in a very relaxed manner, said he would take care of things. Rupert evidently fluttered down to the woods where the lion was napping after a delicious goat dinner. He explained to the lion the dissonance he was causing in the local neighborhood. Rupert followed up that information with a polite request that the lion please move out of this area.

The lion laughed at Rupert. "Absolutely not. I have found a good area with plenty of prey, and there was no way I would give this up."

Rupert explained to the lion, if he did not take his advice and urging, he would be forced to make him leave.

The lion just laughed at Rupert again. "Go ahead and try. It would be a sad day when a lion was forced to do anything by a butterfly."

Rupert smiled. "Gee, that's too bad. Well, I guess we will have to do it the hard way."

The lion scoffed at Rupert as he fluttered away. In a short while, Rupert was back, flying directly and quickly at the lion's face. Just out of reach, he would veer upward and over the lion, all the while releasing the catnip pollen he had gone to collect. Now if you've ever seen the effects of catnip pollen on cats, you know the effect this had upon this poor lion.

Rupert was relentless. He kept coming back with more catnip pollen, and after a while, the poor lion was just plain goofy. At the point where the large cat had lost his sense of direction and purpose, Rupert began to give strong directions to the circus animal. He did this by withholding the next dose of catnip until the lion complied with his directions. It was a simple case of conditioning, and it was not long before Rupert was in total control. Rocko's grandfather evidently had a very strong sense of humor and irony.

It was not enough that he led the big cat back to the circus and captivity, but he felt the need to sort of show off his control in the situation. He walked the cat back through the barnyard, fluttering overhead, giving directions, and withholding the catnip as a control technique. It was obviously an attempt to show off his control in the situation to the other animals. He even got the circus animal to perform a few tricks for the animals in the barnyard.

This was an enormous boast to his reputation and animals, both wild and domesticated, talked about this incident for years afterward. The greatest irony to the life of Rupert, however, was how he eventually met his fate. He was feeding on pollen from some low-hanging flowers when a house cat took him out. Some said it was a type of justice for not being kinder and more humble to his large circus cousin.

Goner the Goose

34

I'd like to tell you just a brief history of Goner the Goose. Now I know I've mentioned it before, but I just want to remind you how Goner got his name. His actual birth name was Anthony, but Goner was forever getting into dicey, dangerous situations where onlookers always commented "He's a goner." His reputation for involving himself in conflict that he could not possibly win was common knowledge.

Hearing about these stories secondhand made me curious to find out about this interesting animal. I went over to the barnyard last Tuesday and saw Goner engaged in a friendly conversation with some other geese. I introduced myself and asked Goner if he would give me some time to interview him. This request must have seemed strange to Goner because he looked at me like I was trying to start a fight. Knowing his track record, I immediately qualified my request with some positive comments about his fame in the barnyard.

This seemed to please Goner, and his attitude changed like the sun coming out after a summer rain. "The thing of it is," said Goner, "I was raised to always think in terms of contributing to society and having a positive effect on those around me."

"That's not what he did when he picked a fight with the pigs," said a swan, who was sort of listening in on our conversation. "He started yelling at the pigs for slopping their mud bath up onto the common run where all the other animas had to pass."

"What happened there?" I asked Goner.

He was about to answer when the swan cut him off and described how the pigs had rolled even closer to him getting him all muddy and irritated. Goner, said the swan, went into full battle formation and charged into the pig's mud bath. The swan stated with a degree of wonderment that everyone watching thought Goner was a goner for sure this time as the pigs rolled over him in their mud bath. He managed to survive this fiasco, but not without receiving a first-class mud bath that took days to get totally off him.

Goner dismissed this story telling, as if the swan had been talking about someone else. Goner slipped back into our conversation like it was an old shoe. "That's what formed my identity. I always thought of myself as trying to add value to anything I was involved in. That identity was how I lived."

"That's not what he did when he picked a fight with the horses," said an old mule who had been silently listening to our exchange.

Goner flashed an irritating look toward the mule.

"The horses were going down the run toward the pasture when one of them left manure on the run," said the mule. "Well, Goner took offense and charged into the horses' ranks, honking and complaining like he was the king of England. The horses were caught off guard and started to kick and rear up, and everyone watching said, with Goner there under all those hooves, he was a goner for sure."

"He managed to survive that incident," said a chicken who was sitting on a fence post next to the mule. "He looked like he went through a wind tunnel, and his honking was off-key for about a month, but gradually he returned to what he called normal."

Goner looked at me and appeared to be organizing his thoughts. "The thing is that my desire to contribute and add value is gone. It's not like I'm antisocial or anything, but my desire to feel engaged with the community has left the building. It's so different from where I've been that I feel lost."

"He sure didn't act that way when he caused all the goats to stampede," said a duck named Judy.

Goner looked at the duck like he was trying to get rid of a headache. Judy described how Goner had taken offense at some silly nonsense the goats had directed at him. He had lowered his neck and charged into the flock of goats. The goats, who are skittish animals anyway, had all retreated against the shed, and when they found no exit there, they turned and charged in the opposite direction.

Judy sort of shook her head and laughed when she said, "The herd of goats all trampled poor Goner, who was coming from the opposite direction. We all thought he was a goner for sure that time." Judy sort of giggled. "Goner looked like he'd been hung out and beaten like a rug, but he survived and was back in action in a few weeks."

Goner looked at me as if to say that these interruptions had nothing to do with him. "Now the thing I'm trying to describe here is that I feel a bit lost. I have no purpose."

This was an interesting interview, I thought, *because so far I had not asked even one question.*

"I'm not sure what you're trying to tell me," I said to Goner.

"He should tell you he's glad to be alive," said Bowser the Dog.

Goner was trying to speak, but Bowser cut him off and started to describe an incident at milking time in the barn.

"Goner was walking along behind the cows as they were being milked, and one of them passed gas as he was walking by," said Bowser. "Goner took it as a personal affront and started to complain loudly to the cow who was being milked at the time. She put up with it until Goner was just behind her back legs, and she let go a kick that could stagger a stump. Goner was not right for about a month after that, and everyone was surprised when he seemed to get his wits back. I'm surprised that the kick didn't kill Goner."

"Look," I said, "it just seems to me that everyone tells stories about you that describe you as reckless and fearless to the point of placing yourself in danger."

"Yeah," said Goner, "those were the good ol' days when I cared about things. I don't know if it's just me getting older or I've got too many hooves to the head."

"You mean to say," I said, "that you are different than all these stories described."

Goner looked at me like he had the weight of the world on his shoulders. "Don't you see that there is a difference between the public image and the private one?"

"Yes," I said, "but who do I believe? I mean, there is quite a bit of anecdotal information that you really do behave in sort of a reckless way."

"Well," said Goner, "I'm the one having these experiences, so shouldn't you get your information from the source? The most important fact here is that I can't quite get back to the point of caring about anything."

While we were standing there, debating Goner's finer qualities, a whole row of Red's hens came by, heading toward the barn and the promise of some extra feed. Marlene, who was leading the pack, made a snide comment about Goner's sanity as she was going by. Goner heard the comment, lowered his head down, and charged the row of hens honking and cursing the chicken species.

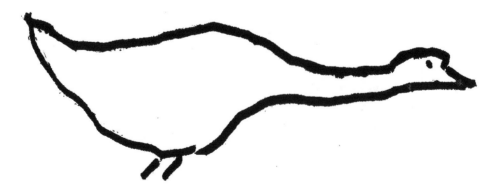

I watched this conflict and thought, *Well, I guess it's good that Goner got over his existential crisis.*

Thores

Sometimes the ordinary is the most amazing. I think this was the case with Rocko the Mean Butterfly. Now everyone I ever talked to in the barnyard sort of knew this. It did not really register with me until I had this conversation with Red the Rooster and Rocko the Mean Butterfly. I suspect that the story I'm about to pass on to you, which Rocko told because of Red's gentle prodding and delicate questions, probably would not have been heard except for Rocko's relaxed relationship with Red and the rooster's unique ability to draw this story from Rocko's otherwise stoic nature.

The conversation began with the question by Red of why butterflies had such amazing qualities. Rocko's one-word answer, "panspermia," left many more questions hanging in the air. A goat nearby asked if this was frying something in a pan.

"No," said Rocko, "it's how the butterflies became the marvelous creatures they are today."

Red the Rooster always knew exactly how to proceed in situations like this. He simply asked Rocko what that was and inquired if he would elaborate a bit about it. This was just the type of relaxing situation a storyteller like Rocko needed to advance his narrative. Rocko began by saying that this happened long before the feeding hands existed on the earth.

"Panspermia is the belief," said Rocko, "that spores or bacteria are carried to our planet from outer space, and that is how life was started on Earth. That's not what happened at all. The truth is much more amazing. What really happens is that galactic winds blow Thores through the universe."

"What are Thores?" a number of the barnyard animals asked simultaneously. They had all begun to collect and listen to this emerging tale.

"Thores are the jellyfish of space," said Rocko. "They are translucent, transparent, evanescent creatures that live in outer space. Thores are interesting creatures. They can survive for a millennial while being blown by these otherwise invisible winds of space. They mate when they meet each other in space by happenstance, which is a million-to-one odds, and they are true hermaphrodites. These meetings are rare, but when they occur, they create millions of Thores who go on to roam the universe, spreading life and knowledge wherever they go."

"Well, what's the connection between Thores and butterflies?" asked a pig who had listened patiently to Rocko's story.

"Many years before the feeding hands learned to walk upright," said Rocko, "the butterflies were simple insects beginning to populate this planet. They had learned to evolve and succeed in a difficult and dangerous environment. Our numbers increased along with the expansion in the number and variety of flowers.

"During these simple times, a Thore was blown onto the earth, and miracle of miracles, blew against a butterfly. This knowledge or story has been handed down verbally through uncounted generations. When Thores are blown against something, they seed life. If the thing they are blown against is already alive, they seed knowledge and the story of life. Now on one hand, this was an amazingly fortuitous and happy accident for the butterflies."

"How did the Thore tell the butterfly what it knew?" asked a duck who was spellbound by Rocko's story.

"That's the amazing part of this story," said Rocko. "You see, when a Thore is blown against a living thing, it gives itself totally to that life-form. A Thore is almost invisible in our atmosphere. It wraps itself around the life-form it touches and melts into that living thing. In that process of symbiosis, it transmits all its information and knowledge into the living thing it has merged with."

"What did it tell the butterfly?" queried a goat.

"Well," said Rocko, "it wasn't so much what it told the butterfly as much as what the butterfly knew after that experience. Now remember, at this point, it was only one butterfly who received this information, so it took generations for this knowledge to spread to the rest of the butterfly population."

"How did it change the butterflies?" asked a pig thoughtfully.

"It transformed them dramatically," said Rocko. "The largest and most powerful change was that they became the arbitrators for the rest of the animals. It was not that they sat in judgment or anything like that. It was simply that they looked after the other animals and helped them through difficult times. Knowledge is power, and it was paradoxical that one of the most fragile creatures became the smartest."

It was interesting at this point in the story because the barnyard animals all knew Rocko, and this caused a subtle surge of agreement among the animals present. This in and of itself was an uncanny verification of the story as well as the power and abilities of butterflies in general.

"What happened to the Thore who gave the butterfly this information?" asked a goose who had followed Rocko's story.

"It's part of the legend," said Rocko, "that, when the butterfly absorbed all the Thore had to offer, the Thore became even lighter and was blown back into space. There in the emptiness of space, he was recharged again with the knowledge of life. We the butterflies don't pretend to understand that, but we do know that the parting of the Thore was marked by a jubilant celebration because the butterflies at that point graduated to a new status in the animal kingdom."

"What now?" asked a horse, who everyone could see had been visibly moved by Rocko's story.

"Well," said Rocko, "it's supposedly true that a Thore can always visit or revisit any planet or animal anywhere in the universe."

"Will it always be the same information that is exchanged?" asked a cow.

"Oh no," said Rocko. "The thing is the universe is always learning lots more things, and the Thores are there to communicate it back and spread it around."

"Wow!" said a turkey. "That's an amazing story. It sort of changes the way we look at our world that we live in."

"Yes," said Rocko, "the Thores have a saying among themselves."

"What's that?" asked a mule, who usually was not even drawn into groups like this.

"Well," said Rocko, "they say to be patient because eventually we'll get to everyone."

Vanity Before the Fall

I t is with some dismay that I have to honestly report an injury to one of our main characters. Now it's true that the injury was mostly to his image, but nevertheless this type of comeuppance is difficult for someone like Red the Rooster to endure. The initial cause for this narrative began quite a while ago, and no one at the time realized what was happening.

What occurred was that the feeding hands left the farmer's almanac in the barn. They were always referring to books because they are, I guess, so poor at intuiting life. They are not very good at figuring things out for themselves, so they always have to have these books around. Anyway, on the cover of this year's copy of the almanac was a picture of a rooster standing on the roof of a barn crowing.

Red the Rooster saw this and was totally captivated by the idea. Now it had always been part of Red's daily routine to wake up the barnyard with his morning crowing. He usually did this up near the barn, which he felt was sort of the center of the barnyard and gave everyone equal opportunity to hear his beautiful crowing. No one had ever complained that they didn't hear him while many paid him extravagant praise for his morning wake-up call.

Reconstructing Red's thought process after seeing this picture of the rooster on the roof of the barn went something like this, *Everyone will be able to hear me better, and I'll cut quite an image standing there on the roof, inviting the morning into the barnyard.* Ideas are always easy to navigate while reality has a much steeper slope. Nevertheless Red decided that his wake-up call would be made each morning from the pinnacle of the barn roof.

This was actually a great idea. Idea was the main focus, if not to say the weak theme there. In reality it had problems. One was that the metal barn roof was very steep. This made getting up there just a bit of a problem. Not only was the steep roof difficult to gain traction on, the metal surface was impervious to Red's talons. Red was not one, however, to be easily discouraged by a few obstacles.

Red approached this challenge by jumping onto the highest post of the fence near the barn. From there he leaped onto the shed roof attached to the barn. At that point Red would get a fast run up the lower part of the barn roof, flapping his vestigial wings to create as much lift as possible. A number of times he would have to repeat this part of the effort to gain the upper barn roof because he would end up sliding back down on to the shed roof.

Once he did gain successfully the upper barn roof, however, he had to run laterally across this upper roof while inching upward as he traversed the length of the barn. He only learned this technique to mount the barn after repeated attempts.

Now you would think that the inherent danger and difficulty involved in this effort would have discouraged any normal rooster. Red was special and made of sterner stuff. The mere fact that he figured out how to accomplish this task was, he thought, proof enough that he was on the right track. The image in his mind of himself crowing from the peak of the roof seemed like destiny calling. Red was not to be denied.

Difficult though it was, Red made his morning crow every morning thereafter from the top of the barn. It did resonate to the surrounding area with a resonance that bordered on beautiful. He received many compliments from the other barnyard animals. He was even heard down the road at nearby farms. Red was right about one thing, the image and acoustics of his crowing from atop the barn was memorable beyond description.

Red felt as if he had turned a corner of creativity and notoriety in regards to this task he owned as one of his main responsibilities. I guess, because of this feeling, Red began to take special care to express his crowing with thoughtful intensity and focus. Now it's always true that mastering one task can leave another chore wanting cynosure. Unfortunately this other task was hanging on to the roof as he crowed one morning.

It happened about a week after he started his morning crowing from on top of the barn roof. He was standing there on the peak. He had flapped his wings a couple times to gain a more robust lung full of air, and he was midway into a beautiful crow when his talons slipped on the metal surface of the roof.

A master stays focused. Red continued his morning announcement even as he lost his balance on the peak and began to slide down the front of the roof where there was no shed roof to break his fall.

It was not until he went flying off the top roof onto the steeper roof that a fearful gurgle of despair broke the cadence of the crow. Red's wings were moving faster than a turbine, and the crowing had disintegrated into an incomprehensible chortle. There was a loud thud when Red hit the ground. He had managed to break his fall by using his wings the way his ancestors had. It was not perfect, but falling from the roof had triggered a memory he didn't even know was there. He got to his feet and discovered that the main injury was to his dignity.

There is an old saying, "Hit your head and change your life." Now Red's epiphany came from a good wallop to his whole body. The ache in his body lasted for weeks after this fall. The insight was a bit more permanent. Red realized the image of himself on the roof was a fantasy chased away initially by the ache in his body but more timelessly by the damage delivered to his vanity. Another way to say this was his memory became his honest friend. Red realized his morning crowing did not have to have heroic aspirations but rather a steadfast, unwavering delivery.

The other animals in the barnyard followed this story with intense interest without speaking about it above a whisper. The communication about it took place clandestinely in small groups out of earshot of Red. This apparently left the little dignity that was left for Red in place. He continued his morning crowing from atop the fence post next to the barn but never attempted to regain the high heights of the barn roof again. Some animals did comment that his crowing took on a maturity and contained a wisdom heretofore missing in the previous morning announcements.

It was also suggested that there was a new profundity and philosophical quality to his morning community ritual. The farmer's almanac did go missing, however.

Red and Rocko's Field Trip

Anybody can tell a story about somebody, but finding the truth of the matter is the hard part in reporting things. I have meticulously practiced this trait in reporting the affairs of both Red the Rooster and Rocko the Mean Butterfly. Sometimes I hear stories about these characters, and I have not been on-site to check the validity of what really happened. It is just such a case that I wonder about reporting to you because I was not there and do not know what really happened.

Now considering that, let me tell you a story I heard that is worth telling, if only to enhance the reputations of these larger-than-life characters. You will have to go elsewhere to verify the truth of these events. It all supposedly started when Rocko was telling Red about the great adventures and excitement in being a nondomesticated animal.

Red, a free-range chicken, has had plenty of adventures all on his own. I suppose it was this very appetite for adventure, however, that teased Red into accepting Rocko's offer to come with him as he surveyed wild animal habitats. Rocko told Red that he would be surprised to see that wild animals generally got along as well as domesticated animals, up to and until they got hungry. Then all bets were off, and pandemonium could break out.

The way this habitat survey worked was that Rocko would guide Red from the air, telling him where and when to move through the fields and woods. The point was to keep Red, a domesticated chicken and an easy meal for some of the wild animals, out of sight so he could see the sights without becoming prey for any of Rocko's wild cousins. For a while, this worked fine.

Rocko showed Red the beaver dam and explained how beavers worked with many other animals in the vicinity. He showed Red how the deer alerted other animals when danger came into the area. He told Red how the wolves performed a function for smaller animals by teaching them to stay close to their dens and secure places when larger predators passed through their area.

I guess things were going along fine. Red was having a great time and following Rocko's directions until a chicken hawk, high above and out of sight, began watching this guided tour. It might have been a form of arrogance on Rocko's part that he didn't realize there could be an unseen predator out of his game plan. Now chicken hawks have that name for a reason, and it's not because they look like chickens.

Rocko was guiding Red over a hill to show him a bear den when suddenly the chicken hawk dove down toward Red. If it had been any other chicken besides Red, he would have ended up on the dinner menu of this flying predator. At the last moment, Red saw the shadow of this airborne warrior and went into his fighting posture, surprising and disrupting the hawk's initial attack.

The attack had just begun. But little did this airborne killing machine realize, this innocent-looking, domesticated chicken had an ally within helping distance. Rocko saw the initial attack, and although he was caught off guard at first, he sprang into action. He quickly flew in a circle around Red, about five feet off the ground, flapping his wings in a very distinctive way. The hawk was quick to return to his attack.

This time, however, he found that he flew into a heavy cloud of ragweed pollen just above Red. Most people don't know it, but chicken hawks are very allergic to ragweed. Rocko knew this and saw an opportunity once he realized that Red was walking through a large patch of ragweed. Butterflies have the ability to draw pollen into the air from many kinds of plants, but it is especially easy for them to create a cloud of ragweed pollen, as he had just done.

The attacker had lost his advantage and landed, congested and coughing, a short way off from Red. Now that he was on the ground, the two birds were on equal terms. Red became the attacker. The hawk turned and saw Red coming through his bleary, swollen eyes. Red began pecking at the hawk's feet as he took off. Evidently Red could not help it. He started crowing loudly and flapping his wings. This ample display was something new in the wild, and all the wild animals in the vicinity went "Huh!" Then they settled back into their normal daily activities.

Now there was just a bit of irony in this tale because Rocko heard from some of the chicken hawk friends that the hawk was very put out at Rocko for helping a domesticated rooster against one of his wild, flying cousins. Rocko was never one to deny good friendships and came to Red's defense with an explanation of their deep and longtime relationship. The wild, or nondomesticated, animals have a strong deference to "what is," so that was that. Besides everyone knew the chicken hawk was just terribly embarrassed over the whole event and wanted to focus everyone's attention elsewhere.

I'm not sure why, but this story circulated wildly with all the animals in the barnyard. So in my mind, it began to take on the feel of gossip. And everyone knows that the most destructive force affecting the truth is gossip. With this in mind, I must caution readers to fact-check this story on their own. I'm also suspicious because, for as long as I've followed Red's and Rocko's exploits, I've never found them to brag or look for notoriety from their escapades. I must honestly report that in this case, that pattern was not followed.

Rocko and Red were sitting off to the side in the barnyard. Their bellies were sore from laughing.

Rocko said, "Now it's agreed. You can't tell anyone, okay?"

"Agreed," said Red. "The joke is just between us."

The chicken hawk flew over the barnyard, and both Red and Rocko acknowledged him with a nod of approval. After that episode, Red was taken much more seriously whenever he was called upon to settle arguments in the barnyard.

Spring Comes to the Henhouse

Well, here I am again with essentially nothing to say of great import, but I did hear some rumors from the henhouse that I think are interesting to pass on. Now I don't want you to think I'm a busybody just trafficking in gossip. It seemed to me to be the kind of goings-on that any curious and intelligent person would be interested in. What I heard was that Red the Rooster was just about beside himself because the hens had gotten cabin fever so bad. The snow this season had been more than usual, and along with the abundant snow, there was also a persistent cold that kept the chickens all inside their coop. Now this had gone on for over a month and a half, and while that coop was still his domain, Red began to feel that it was indeed more like a prison.

The hens had been arguing and getting in each others' business so bad that it made that relatively small chicken coop a chaotic and hectic environment to say the least. Red, I guess, had tried to calm things down with his usual strategy of prancing up and down and back and forth, all the time crowing and puffing out his chest so as to impress and intimidate the hens into being a good clutch. Well, that didn't work so well in such a small place as the chicken coop and was much better theatre in a place like the open barnyard. And truth be told, the hens were suffering the same claustrophobia and dystonia that was shoving Red toward the edge of his sanity.

It actually came to the point where poor Red overheard some of the hens making jokes about his manly behavior. It was to the point of saying his behavior was a parable without a point. That just devastated poor Red, but he was way too proud to admit his symbolic downfall and took up his station on the highest roost and continued to play the role of protector and procreator. Now on the inside, poor Red, I guess, felt like he had been wounded and piteously hurt. The larger truth was that it was only his self-image that had been mauled a bit, but other than that, things remained the same. Now all this was occurring while watching with dismay the increasing reign of chaos as it continued to reach new heights and intensities inside the coop.

Not that it's even worth reporting, but Lucy claimed that Georgia had taken over a nest where she had just laid two fresh eggs. Marlene said that Ruth had taken a bunch of straw from her nest and not replaced it. And Mable and Josephine were just clucking nasty nonsense at each other on a regular schedule. And there were lesser arguments that I won't even bother going into. Red's nerves were not only stretched to the breaking point but inflamed and irritated to the point that he felt like crying. Now that's saying something when the hens had brought Red to that point.

Red had tried everything. He got the hands that filled the feeding bins to play classical music for the hens, and this did work until the hens started to fight about which piece of music was best and which allowed for the largest production of eggs. It was like trying to keep track of the bubbles in boiling water.

Red was getting a very large headache. He asked the feeding hands to supply more and different food, but it turned out to just be another reason or something to fight about. Red thought about Rocko the Mean Butterfly and wondered if he would know what to do, but that was all hypothetical because, of course, Rocko was thousands of miles away on his yearly migration journey. Red thought, *Lucky him.*

Red was tough, if nothing else, and settled in for the long haul. You know the old saying that the tough get going when the going gets tough. He continued to mediate arguments in a fair and reasonable way, he settled disagreements, and he tried to maintain a pleasant and chicken-friendly atmosphere in the coop. While his headaches continued and his nerves remained frayed, Red plowed on in his best rooster fashion.

The cold, snow, and winter dragged on. Red held to the idea, "It may look as if the situation is creating the suffering, but ultimately this is not so. Your resistance is." He tried to be paternal and loving. The days dragged on. And then one day, he got a hint of it. It wasn't much, just a slight hint. Spring might come after all.

At first it was just a slight promise on a shadow. There was a tiny, brief light where there had been none before, hardly noticeable to one who had not been mauled by the long winter. To Red it was like a neon sign had been installed around it. He didn't need attention to be drawn to it. It had its own pulsing life. Not much yet, but it was there, alive and promising more life. It had the potential of an explosion. A wonderful warm, promising thing entered his consciousness. The first slight suggestion of spring appeared.

It was always interesting when this first occurred because initially really nothing happened. It was like something invisible touched you and at first you didn't understand it. The awareness happened deep within your body, and it delighted in the promise it was given. Later as the process of spring progressed, that feeling was shared to the rest of your consciousness, and indeed eventually it affected your body as well.

There was gladness in Red's heart for the coming event. These feelings belong to all creatures that suffer the long winter. These descriptions also don't do these feelings that overtakes us justice in springtime. It was somewhat like trying to describe the first time you tasted ice cream or rode a roller coaster. The thing is, though, spring fever is different from any other feeling. It is a unique experience that all living creatures are vulnerable to. Mama Earth and all her manifestations turn strongly again toward life. We belong to her and are brought along forcefully. Something deep inside of us wakes up, and you see in a sideway glance that your body is the placenta for your soul.

It was one of those wonderful spring days. The hens were all out in the barnyard, scratching and moving about. The sun was warming up everything. Red was surveying his domain. All was right with the world. Red looked up and saw Rocko the Mean Butterfly fluttering overhead. He thought, *He can't really know spring without the trials of winter.*

Rocko, for his part, looked down and saw the chickens milling about in the small barnyard. He thought, *Chickens are weird. They enjoy the strangest things.*

Jeremy and Rocko

I know in the past I've told you about the water hole and the characters that gather there for water or social contact. The one figure I've neglected to describe in detail is the large bullfrog who is a constant presence there. Now this was not an oversight on my part. Jeremy the Bullfrog is actually quite a powerful, wise, and remarkable animal. I've always been careful about describing Jeremy because of the relationship between him and Rocko the Mean Butterfly.

The two of them have always been just a bit at odds with each other. The reason for the conflict actually goes back generations in butterfly lives. I only know this much because Red has told me a bit about it. Although the initial issues and instigating cause for their disagreement is, as they say, ancient history, the part I'm aware of is their attitudes and behavior toward each other in the present. There is—and never has been any—actual open conflict between them.

Actually they treat each other with gratuitous respect. It's like they really defer to each other and pay a grudging tribute to the other's talents. However, they are cold, distant, and almost openly hostile toward each other. It's a weird relationship, and everyone in the barnyard is aware of it. I was also a player in this strange liaison. I did not pretend to any friendship there or the possibility of any type of communication. It was because of this established entente and my closer relationship with Rocko, that I never cultivated a relationship with Jeremy the Bullfrog.

Now last Tuesday in a conversation between Red, Rocko, and some of the cows, Rocko offhandedly quoted Jeremy as a source of insight about relationships between animals. I think one of the cows actually pooped right there on the spot. There were sly glances all around among everyone except Rocko. Red actually started to cough to cover up his surprise, which didn't work at all because chickens don't usually cough like that anyway. Needless to say, it was a pregnant moment. No one knew quite what to think.

That particular gathering broke up a little after that, and everyone went their own way, seething with theories about what had happened in the relationship between Jeremy and Rocko. If indeed this represented some type of détente between these two, this then was big news in the barnyard. Well, as you can well imagine, the gossip mill went into overdrive, and the doubt created by Rocko's initial comment was carried right along with it. Everyone was asking everyone what the others thought about it.

Now just to give you the flavor of those interactions, I've documented a few of those interchanges here. George the Pig, who liked to philosophize, told some of the sheep that it was like east meeting west. Except in this case, it was wild and domesticated coming to a new rapprochement. I overheard one of the goats telling the ducks it was because Rocko was afraid Jeremy would hold him underwater when he went for a drink at the water hole. Some of the swans had the idea and were telling anyone who would listen that Rocko wanted to explore and learn about the underwater world. There was just a plethora of theories about the thaw in this relationship.

It was actually quite amusing that no one thought to ask either Jeremy or Rocko about their relationship. It was just assumed, because of their stature and reputation, that both Rocko and Jeremy were the last to be consulted about the nature and quality of their affiliation. Marlene, one of Red's hens, made the obvious comment as everyone was settling down for the night in the coop. She had been listening to various theories and comments about this connection or lack of it and was growing weary of the sameness of it all.

"Why doesn't somebody ask either Jeremy or Rocko what's going on?" she inquired.

The clutch was stunned into silence, as was the barnyard the following day. Of course, as always, Red was asked to do the hard part. It took a bit of badgering, but he knew right off that he would end up being the one who asked the hard questions. I thought it interesting, however, that he approached Jeremy first. Now frog speak is not a difficult dialect to translate, and Red had enough experience with various tongues that he could manage this.

He reported back his conversation with Jeremy that evening, and it was a bit befuddling to everyone gathered there in the barnyard. Jeremy said he knew nothing about a relaxation in the relationship between him and Rocko.

He added, "I respect Rocko immensely, even though he is an arrogant, dogmatic, opinionated, stuffed shirt who can't tell water from land."

I guess that last part is very insulting for amphibians, telling water from land. Anyway it did not take a sharp measuring tool to see that the melt in the interrelationship did not come from Jeremy.

Red bumped into Rocko the very next day, so the questions were posed anew. Everyone stayed clear as they saw this conversation taking place. They did not want to jinx it in any way.

Later that day Red went up toward the barn and was immediately followed by a large crowd who wanted to know. They gathered around Red before he even had a chance to turn and call the barnyard meeting to order.

"Nothing's changed," he said. "Rocko and Jeremy are as they have always been. It's just that Rocko sees that having a resource like Jeremy in the community and not taking advantage of his knowledge and wisdom is foolish."

Rocko said, "Jeremy and I do not have to be friends in order to recognize the beauty, quality, and goodness to his way of life. In addition, if our dispute interfered with Jeremy's ability to contribute to the larger community, it was his responsibility to break the emotional logjam and allow things to change."

This was just a bit anticlimactic after all the speculation that had gone before. A lot of the animals had quite expected something different. Mostly they didn't understand Rocko's announcement.

Two goats walking away were heard to say, "Why does that bullfrog always want to rip stuff up?"

"What do you mean?" asked the other goat.

The first goat responded, "I hear him say each evening, 'Ribbit-ribbit.' I just assume he's an anarchist and wants to rip something up."

Things returned to normal quite quickly. The only difference was a slight warning of the relationship between Rocko and Jeremy. Jeremy continued his nightly prayer each evening of ribbit-ribbit, but really you have to speak frog to understand what he was saying.

Gruff

It's not often that the farmyard gets a visitor that will eventually leave. Gruff the Bull from a neighboring farm was in that category. He was just temporarily here for his inherent skills. No one knew for sure how long he would be here, but the one thing they did realize was that he made a deep impression. Gruff was an amazing animal by any measurement. Let me just describe his credentials.

Gruff was almost thirty-two hundred pounds of muscle. He had large, protruding horns that looked very intimidating. He walked through the barnyard, and everyone just stopped and stared. It was like watching a super athlete with well-trained muscles quietly make a commanding statement. Gruff had an air about him that just commanded respect not only because of his size and strength but also because of his demeanor.

Now here's the curious part to this description. Gruff was as gentle as can be. He had not a mean bone in his body. The massive potential for destruction in his body had never been used. Gruff was not only gentle but kind and timid to boot. On top of that, it appeared that he liked who he was and was willing to share that with his fellow animals. It was a case where looks betrayed reality. Gruff was completely unable to hurt anyone. He stood in obvious contradiction to what he looked like. The thing was that no one could know that by just looking at him. There was a real learning curve in getting to know Gruff.

You might well imagine the initial impression of apprehension that Gruff created when he arrived at the barnyard. Unlike other bulls before him, he was not staked to a limited area but left to graze the pasture at will. This initially created just a bit of a problem. The other animals who grazed there were a bit reticent to enter the pasture and graze next to Gruff. Unknown to Gruff, he was watched like he was a celebrity for the first day that he was in the meadow.

There were a sufficient number of conversations all about if it was safe to graze in the pasture next to Gruff. The first hint of any hazard regarding Gruff was disclosed when everyone watched some songbirds alight on his horns and sing their songs. Mildred the Mare took the next step and really broke the ice by going into the meadow and quietly grazing. The observation was immediately made that, not only did it appear safe, Gruff politely and warmly acknowledged Mildred. He did that by staying off her usual run and not grazing across her path or direction. Yes, animals have grazing etiquette, rules that keep conflict and dissension to a minimum.

The other animals took note of the adaptation among these animals and understood that there was no danger in grazing with Gruff. It followed shortly that the pasture filled up with all the usual animals that browsed there. They took to the meadow in increasing numbers as it became obvious that there was no threat or danger. Everyone relaxed, and indeed the presence of Gruff added another pleasant quality to the farmland.

Time and closeness create certain amity. This happened quite quickly with Gruff. What initially had been so frightening and intimidating now became the fuel for camaraderie and concord. His very size as an issue became a protection against anything else in the world. Instead of a threat, he was viewed as an ally. Now anyone observing this could easily see that all of this had transpired in the minds of the farm animals exclusive of Gruff. Gruff himself remained at first unaffected and really somewhat unaware of this whole transformation in the minds of his fellow farm animals.

Now just as the interactions between neurons define us as individuals, the exchanges between individuals create the community. It is the content and intent of those exchanges then that is so important. We defer to those that are bigger and stronger. It is part of our history to do so. Gruff became easily and without effort an authority figure. That in its turn began to define the community. There was no good or bad to this. It was just so.

Well, you can well imagine that the deference created by Gruff's size was really a creation inside the minds of his fellow animals. It does not take long, however, for this energy to ricochet back to the object creating this force. Gruff began to understand his role in the community. Initially he had no idea what to do with all this power. It seemed to him as well as the other animals as this progressed that he was just wealthy with authority. There is an old proverb among the butterflies, "Life makes fools of us all."

Maybe that's what happened, or maybe just no one was paying close enough attention. Anyway the subtle virus of authoritarianism was planted. Now the really curious thing about this is not that it makes anyone do anything, but rather how it starts to change the way everyone thinks. The nature of the mind is a prison, especially when the belief exists that an authority will have the last say.

Things slowly began to change. At first it really was not even noticeable and, if noted, was easily condoned because everyone simply agreed to it. The flower of thought was replaced by a certain nod to the crowd's contagion. Someone would shout something, and the throng took up the chorus. It was not that anyone tried to sway the assemblage. It was more a matter of going with the flow. Everyone simply liked being part of the larger enthusiasm. It was an escape out of the self into the body politic. Everyone felt like they were part of something bigger.

In a windstorm the leaves in a tree do not disparage the other leaves for the thrashing they take. Unfortunately a community does not operate quite that way. The goats had a complaint. They said the pigs encroached upon their pen after their mud baths, and it left mud everywhere.

They were terribly indignant about all of this and took it to Gruff to see if he would settle the matter. Gruff did not have many management skills, but he did have a lot of authority. Gruff scolded the pigs and told them not to go next to the goat pen after their mud baths.

The pigs heard a criticism of their very nature and felt, in this instance, excluded and ostracized via Gruff's commands. Pigs are very intelligent and have a strong community within their own ranks. The idea of dissension and revolution did not take long to form. Pigs actually have better language skills than most other animals, and they began to enlist some of the other barnyard animals into their point of view.

It was not long before open conflict began to be the potential in the barnyard. Disagreements fueled by hate became the order of the day. Right in the middle of all this, Gruff returned to his original farm. It caught everyone off guard. Everyone stopped and looked at what was happening in the barnyard. There was a deep amount of embarrassment. Things eventually returned to normal, and certain animals said they had learned something. That, however, remained to be seen.

Flip and Flop

I was over at the barnyard the other day, and the talk going round was about Flip and Flop, the two squirrels that live in the tree in front of the barn. I guess they had been running around the inside of the barn and chasing each other like squirrels often do, and it was aggravating some of the barnyard animals. Most of the animals don't make a steep distinction between wild and domesticated if the animals generally get along. The thing with the squirrels is that they often don't respect the spaces of the barn animals, and they can be quite annoying.

The cows don't like being surprised by fast-running rodents, and it can interfere with their milk production. The horses as well have a quiet, passive disposition and don't like being jolted into reality by these squirrels running under their feet. In addition to that, the goats go daft when these guys startle them. It's not a species problem as much as a generational one. These squirrels are youngsters and full of playfulness. They are just doing what comes natural to them.

It's interesting because generally most of the barnyard animals enjoy watching the squirrels chase each other relentlessly. They really are a show all by themselves. I guess the catch is when they run into and out of the barn where the cows, horses, and goats are stabled. Now some of the talk is interesting because I've heard it said that, if you take away their bushy tails, they're really just rats. Not that there is anything wrong with that.

The animals in the barnyard all have strong opinions about this because it directly affects them. The geese have made it a point to not complain about the squirrels publically. They talk about them in a positive way, but when I asked them some pointed questions about the squirrels' behavior, they did say that both Flip and Flop could be annoying at times.

The swans are interesting in this way because they have given chase to the squirrels when they've become too intrusive. I was not there to see this interaction, but it was reported to me that the squirrels kept their distance after that go-round with the swans.

I've already reported what the goats, horses, and cows think about the squirrels so I was a bit surprised that the narrative about Flip and Flop had taken a surprising turn when I visited the barnyard after a short hiatus. Everyone was very upset with both Flip and Flop, although the goats admitted they could not tell which was Flip and who was Flop. I guess in the spirit of play the squirrels had chased each other around the barnyard relentlessly. Still I was taken back by the severity of the comments I overheard regarding them.

The thing about collective opinions that build a crescendo, drawing everyone's thoughts into the stream, is that I don't trust it. I'm not saying that both Flip and Flop are not irritating and aggravating at times, but the storm of thought building against them seemed to have a fabricated quality. In describing the negative, the listener takes it and extrapolates it for the benefit of the new listener. In this way, the story begins to have a life of its own, disconnected from the facts of the matter.

The conversations bubbling into the open in the barnyard about the squirrels' behavior sort of had this quality to it. If someone were off their feed and didn't feel good for whatever reason, it was the fault of these two rascals. Ever the reporter, I made my rounds and listened. Now I won't bore you with the details and content of all these conversations. Suffice it to say, the mob's body exists mostly as opinions without thought. I was curious as to what opinion Red would have about this matter, so I wandered down toward the chicken coop.

Red was sitting on top of his coop and had one eye open while it seemed he was deep in thought with the other eye closed. I was just a bit hesitant to approach him, but once I got within hailing distance, he called out to me. I went over and sat down on the fallen log behind the chicken coop, and Red joined me there shortly thereafter.

"What do you make of the storm of thought about Flip and Flop that is going round the barnyard?" I asked Red.

Red thought for a moment. "The community finds a tyrant in its collective opinions. They all want to feel right, safe, and secure inside this rolling flash of a supposition they've got going by being reckless in thought with each other. It's a virus that flows through the tribe sometimes."

"Well, what is to be done?" I asked. "It really is not fair to the poor squirrels."

"It's much like a grass fire," said Red. "Sometimes it burns itself out all by itself. In other situations it weakens the fabric that holds us together, and using the fire analogy, that's when it burns down our living spaces."

I had never heard Red make such negative predictions and was just a little alarmed by the potential he was describing. "What are you going to do?"

"I've asked for and arranged for a meeting with Rocko the Mean Butterfly," he said. "He has a certain knack and ability to analyze situations like this. Since it is getting on to the fall, the butterflies are preparing for their migration, but Rocko said he would take some time and return to the barnyard to see if he could be of assistance in this matter. He will be here tomorrow morning early, so if you want to come back, you can ask him yourself what's to be done in this situation."

I returned early the next day and went immediately down to the chicken coop, where I found Red and Rocko already deeply involved in a tête-à-tête. I was a bit surprised because Rocko was laughing and seemed totally unconcerned about the whole matter. I did not want to interrupt their conversation, so I waited until they appeared to have finished their colloquy. Red turned to his hens and asked them all to fan out and collect all the barnyard animals down here near his coop for a general meeting.

I was relieved in one way and terribly curious as to what would be said at this meeting. Slowly the animals collected and patiently waited for the proceeding to begin. Finally Red stepped forward and described the aforementioned virus and its negative potential. He then said that Rocko would like to address the community.

Rocko always speaks in a soft manner, so all the animals had to lean in to hear what he was saying. "Just watch the squirrels as they chase each other. No one can play so intensely like that without understanding love. In watching Flip and Flop play and act out their version of love, remember it is that quality that we hold dear in the barnyard."

He said some other things, but the animals disbanded in a bit, and things returned to normal in the barnyard in a very short amount of time after that. There was a new seeing when Flip and Flop chased each other.

Rats in the Barnyard

I want to tell you about what happened in the barnyard last week, but I am a bit reluctant to tell you about the seedier side of that wonderful place. Anyway with that being said and the recognition that you're a bit older now, I guess I can proceed with this type of story.

The barnyard has rats. Yes, it's true. Now the reality of this disturbing situation has a story that perhaps will be a bit upsetting to delicate minds. Down and back of the chicken coop is a hedgerow about twenty feet away from the coop. I'm not sure where they come from or where their domicile is, but every night after dark, a parade of rats comes out of this hedgerow looking for food in the barnyard.

The hens all know about these rats because they pass by the coop just after the chickens have nested for the night. The reason the hens are sort of familiar with these guys is because the rats, as they come out of the hedgerow, are communicating with each other about where to look for food and giving each other directions generally. The hens even know the leaders' names, Vinnie and Angelo, because as the rats enter the barnyard, those two give the directions and manage the foraging trip. The hens can plainly hear these discussions through the thin wall of the chicken coop as the rats begin their foray.

Now there is nothing essentially wrong with rats. That being said, they are not the most endearing creatures in the animal kingdom. That probably captures Red's opinion most accurately of these visitors to the barnyard. Saying that, however, doesn't reveal the whole vision Red has of these nightly marauders. Red is a community guy, and creatures that understand and respect that have his basic acknowledgement.

Rats are a very successful operation in and of themselves. Once they survey the barnyard, they always manage to find something to eat: the splash from the pig trough, the missed feed for the chickens that goes into the higher grasses, or the spillover from the various feeding bins that go uneaten by the several animals it's meant for. To the rats, it's a feast. Now the unwritten truth to survival is no one begrudges the rats their efforts to maintain life and limb.

Now the incident to which I refer began to happen last week after the rats became aware of the chickens listening to their progress into the barnyard. It was probably Denise who could make friends with a chicken mite. She wanders all over and most likely ran into one of these rats during the day and greeted him by name, trying to initiate a friendship. It was not a leap of imagination that the rats realized their operation was not as clandestine as they supposed. The realization of someone listening actually changes your behavior. We think that's what happened in this situation. I talked it over with Rocko the Mean Butterfly and that was his best guess as to what occurred.

The rats after that, as they passed by the chicken coop after dark, would make rude suggestions to the hens. Now I know and understand that the mission of a children's storyteller is to communicate positive information about the world and what happens in it. This was not the kind of information being suggested by these nightly raiders. Some of these comments suggested interspecies love activities. Now even the feeding hands found this type of activity repugnant.

I won't go into detail for the sake of plain decency, but at the same time, I do want to convey how these comments insulted the deep sensitivities of the chicken coop culture. Red, who was also harbored by the thin walls of the same coop, became aware of what was happening as it unfolded. He was insulted and disgusted by these comments. It was not that Red was a cloistered rooster. He knew the world was a complicated and disturbing place. It was just that, now that it had come to his door, he felt it was his responsibility to do something about it.

He met with Rocko the Mean Butterfly because there were a number of questionable issues involved with addressing this situation. The largest of these was when the rats were present in the barnyard. There was, in essence, a type of night-versus-day barrier between chickens and rats. The rats never ventured into the yard during the day. While this made direct communication with the rats difficult, it also, Red felt, gave him the moral high ground to deal with this emergency. I only call it an emergency because of Red's insistence that something needed to be done to communicate to the rats that their values and behavior were unacceptable to the barnyard in general.

Rocko the Mean Butterfly and Red conversed long and hard about the situation for a number of days. Only after intense conversations between these two was a plan constructed and put into operation. Red had to learn to speak rat, which was not a big problem because he had such good command of chicken speak. He was to station himself next to the wall nearest where the rats passed at night and retaliate with loud admonishments of why their comments were despicable.

This initially caught the rats off guard, and their rude insults fell silent. The serene silence was not long, however. The next night, the rats not only returned to their initial disparagements but placed Red into the middle of their fantasy play. He became the central player in their disgusting descriptions of what various animals can do with each other. Red became very upset and took to brooding on his high roost.

Now Red loved his hens, and they also loved him. Marlene, one of his shyest hens, had a suggestion. Marlene was not strong in language knowledge but did have a rather curious command of a strange talent. She could mimic the language of the feeding hands. She could only do short phrases, and there were a few cluck-clucks included, but if you didn't look at her while she did this, you would swear one of those two-legged beasts was present. Her suggestion was to talk to the rats through the wall and convince them that the feeding hands were present. Everyone knew the rats were terribly afraid of the feeding hands.

The next night, Marlene was stationed next to the wall, and when the rats began their virulent pronouncements, she let fly a number of chastisements that stopped them in their tracks. She followed her initial statements with comments about extermination of their species and various ways to do just that. The rats stopped their rude critiques and actually stopped their forays into the barnyard for quite some time. Whenever they returned, Marlene was placed next to the wall and gave them a new scare that kept them not only very quiet but looking elsewhere for their sustenance.

I know this story might be upsetting to some, but it just shows how reality protrudes into such a wonderful place like the barnyard.

Taking Sides

I want to tell you about a conflict that happened in the barnyard and the various sides it created. How Red the Rooster got involved and how the other animals got drawn into this terrible dissension. Now I don't mean to takes sides in this go-round, but one can hardly deal with terrible events such as this without being sadly affected. So I'll try and be neutral in describing this strife.

It was a dark and stormy night. No, it wasn't. It was a beautiful day in the barnyard, one of those days when everything was going along quite smoothly until one of the cows pooped in front of the horses' stall when she was walking by it. Oh, boy. That set things off. Normally that would not have been a problem, but earlier that day, the horses had been irritated by the goats, who had wandered in and eaten some of their straw bedding. It went from bad to worse when the horses complained, and the cows, in their sanctimonious way, not only ignored the horses but actually made fun of them.

Now I don't know if you realize it, but horses do somewhat carry a certain amount of stature in the barnyard. Partly it's because of being the largest animal in the barnyard. Not largest in weight, however. That prize went to the cows. And that was part of the issue brewing that day. The two largest animals were bickering. Now as everyone knows, bickering can lead to bitching, biting, and then blasting. It's simply dangerous when two large animals openly oppose each other and make their disagreement public.

The other animals immediately took notice, and it was not long before it was brought to the attention of Red the Rooster. Now as everyone knew in the barnyard, Red was very good at negotiating conflicts, as he had done just so many times with his hens. Red went up to the barn from the chicken coop with a swagger in his step and an abiding presence in his posture. He got to the open barn door and let out a vociferous rooster crow. It shook the barn with a vibration that made all the swallows take flight from their nests.

All the horses had a deep respect for Red's thoughts and opinions. The conversation went on for quite some time, and after much and varied exchanges, Red was asked to go and talk to the cows. Knowing their temperament, Red declined the crowing and wing flapping but did stride over boldly to where the cows were herded together like a bunch of co-conspirators. He described how he had talked over the situation with the horses and knew, if he did the same with the cows, a very reasonable accommodation could be made to this terrible friction. The cows, who Red knew always had a leaning toward political correctness, shook their heads in that lazy way that they do and assented to his proffered proposal.

Well, it was all going quite according to plan, and Red was feeling like a real diplomat. He brought the negotiation to the point where the horses were agreeable to accepting a simple verbal apology from just one of the cows, and that would be that. It would be poop under the bridge, as it were. If only Red had gotten the cows to name which of their number would do the apology. The cows had a disagreement among themselves, which ended up with them hating the horses twice as much as they did before. *It's funny sometimes how we just want to be mad at someone*, Red thought.

The failure to consolidate the initial agreement made by Red on top of the nasty words to the horses of why that was not going to happen led to a small spark becoming a large blaze very quickly. Not only were they back to where they were before, now there was some nasty exchanges to go with this escalating fracas. On top of that, the cows had pleaded their case to some of the other animals, and now the horses were also lining up advocates on their side of the argument. Red, an astute observer of nature, looked at the emerging situation and thought, *Haters are gonna hate.*

The barnyard became divided between groups arguing over apology versus no apology and between different groups arguing where it was appropriate to poop and who had the right to eat whose bedding. It was a dismal, chaotic situation where animals were spitting venom at each other. If he didn't know better, Red thought everyone was enjoying this go at each other. Anyway that's how it seemed as the situation escalated into open conflict in the barnyard.

He walked back toward the chicken coop, thinking to himself, *This is just as bad as what the feeding hands do. They have established parties whose job it is to disagree with each other. They are forever fighting with each other, and the only thing accomplished is that no one is taking care of business. Oddly enough, various businesses and corporations then feed off the society. It's a free-for-all for the wealthy to make money off the body politic.* Red shook his head in disbelief. He never thought the barnyard would fall as low as to mimic what the feeding hands do.

Red was feeling quite sad and unsuccessful and wandered into the chicken coop as the hens were settling down on their roosts for the night. Red settled into his roost and absentmindedly listened and watched as the nighttime routine transpired. The hens in this process showed love, respect, and consideration for each other. It was just the chicken way. Chickens have a hard time smiling because of their beaks. Red all a sudden knew how to solve the problem between the cows and horses.

The next morning he gathered all the hens together and told them that he had planned an outing to the barn for them. He explained to them that he wanted them to do their normal socializations and interactions in the barn with the other animals. This was code actually for cows and horses, but he didn't bother to explain that part to them.

The hens loved socializing with each other, and that day in the barn with all the room and the different environment, they had a field day. They gossiped, giggled, and gloated over each other and had a grand time just enjoying one another. The horses and cows never knew why their conflict melted away. They worked very hard at trying to remember why they hated each other, but every time they did, it was always interrupted by those stupid chickens laughing and having a good time.

How could anything serious get done with those stupid chickens around? Roosters are very curious creatures. They crow and flap their wings and generally announce their presence in a very obvious way. The other side to their personality is more subtle. They don't take credit for getting things back to normal. It was a dark and stormy night.

No, it wasn't.

The Rabbit in the Birdbath

O nce again I'm in questionable territory. This thing happened at the birdbath, which is behind the feeding hands coop. Now not a lot of the barnyard animals use this facility, but actually some do. Mostly it's the wild birds, but sometimes even some of the ducks, chickens, and geese go around there. The feeding hands throw birdseed on the ground around the birdbath so at times it's quite the gathering place for the flying two-legged creatures.

I won't tease your curiosity any longer. What has been happening is that Rufo the Rabbit has been going up to the birdbath and lying in it. If he did this one time and was seen no more, I guess he could be forgiven. This, however, is not the case. Rufo has been showing up every day at the birdbath. He hops up on the bench next to the birdbath and, from there, splashes into the center of the birdbath there to stay, ignoring all the protests from those who would like to use it as their daily bath and what not.

This has been going on for almost a week now, and the birds and all their cousins are very upset and agitated about it. It has even come to the attention of Rocko and Red, but so far nothing has been done to rectify the situation. It has been of late the main topic of conversation in the barnyard. It was somewhat interesting where the general opinion was regarding Rufo.

Most of the ducks, geese, chickens, and swans think he is a psychotic criminal who should be eliminated from interacting with any of the other animals. The four-legged animals have a less harsh opinion, but they do see Rufo as a bit antisocial and troublesome. The goats are all in a tizzy to agree with the birds in this, but that is because they simply like hating someone every once in a while. It seems to stretch some strange muscle they have.

I listened to all the opinions and observations about this happening but wanted to observe it for myself. Sometimes reality needs verification after so many opinions have manhandled it. So I went up to the birdbath the following day to see for myself. Sure enough, there in the birdbath was Rufo, lying on his back in the water with all four feet in the air. He looked very comfortable and relaxed.

I thought I might have some persuasion skills of my own so I ventured a question, "Rufo, some of the other animals would like to use the birdbath, and you are sort of totally controlling it."

I don't speak real good rabbit, but Rufo left no doubt as to where I could go and what I could do with my opinion. I was very taken back. Usually rabbits are pleasant creatures with somewhat passive personalities. Rufo did not personify this type of personality. Even as I made this observation, Rufo raised his head and told me to get lost.

I must admit here that sometimes I feel a bit like an interloper in the barnyard culture because I'm never totally sure of barnyard etiquette. Anyway, after being cursed and yelled at by a rabbit, I left. Now it's not that I wasn't angry as to how I'd been treated, but I just figured there was a better way to deal with this problem. I was going to talk to both Red the Rooster and Rocko the Mean Butterfly. I was quite sure they'd know what to do in a situation like this.

I found Red down next to the coop and described in great detail the abuse I had suffered at the hands of the rabbit. Sometimes it's very hard to tell what Red thinks, but he did assure me that he would talk the situation over with Rocko the next day when he saw him. I left the barnyard after that feeling like there was somehow more to this than met the obvious eye. I would return the next day to see what Red and Rocko had to say.

The next day I found both Red and Rocko and a small group of animals had collected around them because word had gotten out that they were going to comment on Rufo's behavior.

Rocko started the conversation, "We have to be tolerant of various behaviors from different animals."

Well, you can just imagine that comment didn't sit well with the birds and their two-legged cousins.

A goat asked bluntly, "Why are we letting Rufo the Rabbit get away with bad behavior?"

I saw Rocko exchange a knowing glance in Red's direction. "Okay," he said. "Let me explain what happened to Rufo, and maybe you'll better understand why he's behaving that way. Rabbits have a reputation for finding and enjoying their mates. Rufo was in love with Susan, a very nice lady rabbit, but the only problem was that Susan was not in love with him. He told her he wanted to do to her what spring does to the world. She looked at him like he was quite out of his mind. Falling in love makes one forget the language of reason. This rejection by Susan left Rufo without any logic for living."

"You see," interjected Red, "Rufo has just recently come back out and started to do things. It's always true that the only cure for this malady is movement. We understand that some of his actions seem just a bit antisocial now, but with time he'll come back to his senses and find his place in our community. We are just asking you to give Rufo some time and patience until he works through this problem."

There was silence in the group that had collected to hear Rocko's and Red's talk.

One of Red's hens said, "The poor dear! Maybe we can give him some extra feed or something."

Some of the other hens chimed in, along with some of the ducks and geese. They were all sorry for their initial opinions and wanted to know what they could do to help poor Rufo. I saw another knowing look exchanged between Red and Rocko.

Red spoke up, "Let me explain. Rejection in love creates indifference and apathy, which steals away your motive for living. Rufo is wandering in a wasteland of not wanting. The very fact that he likes the birdbath is a breakthrough, and we should just let him enjoy that until he doesn't anymore. This is one of those cases where you don't have to do anything. Just let him do what he's doing."

Red and Rocko waited as their little lecture began to sink in. Most of the animals seemed to understand the necessity of leaving Rufo to his healing process. The group began to break up, and the various animals began to leave. I heard a goat say to a swan that he still thought that Rufo looked awfully stupid lying on his back in that birdbath.

The swan said in return, "I guess it's difficult when you don't want to do anything. Maybe Rufo will get better doing his thing in the birdbath."

There was a general nod of agreement as the group continued to break up. One of Red's hens made a comment that a visitation by love can leave one truly devastated. Everyone seemed to agree with that and the anger pointed at Rufo evaporated. The barnyard was not immune to the most powerful force in the universe.

Tasks

Red was walking along on the outside parameter of the barnyard. He often did this to keep tabs on everyone. He took notice of all the barnyard animals and knew their whereabouts, but mostly he kept a constant surveillance on his hens. That was just his nature. While on this walk, he inadvertently came upon Rocko cursing at himself.

Red's first instinct was to laugh, but being a diplomatic rooster, he held his breath and watched. Rocko was taking out his bile on himself.

Rocko was saying, "Stuff to do that you have to do that you want to do. It's amazing how much the idea of doing tasks controls our lives."

"Hi, Rocko," said Red. "What's up?"

"I'm mad about all the things I have to do," said Rocko. "I can remember as a small butterfly being frustrated at having to do the necessary task of getting dressed. Well, it kept going and just never seemed to stop. You had to brush your teeth at night. You had to wash your hands before a meal. Rules, rules, rules. When will it ever end?"

Now, dear reader, if I can just beg your indulgence for a moment, I know you know that butterflies don't have hands to wash or clothes to wear. However, since we have given them self-awareness and speech, can we for the sake of the analogy stretch the space within your imagination to also allow them these other feeding hands' qualities? With that small detail of housekeeping out of the way, I'll go forward relating an otherwise totally true story about what happened in the barnyard that day.

Rocko continued to address Red, "I don't have to tell you how this early stuff was only the worm on the hook. Doing tasks was connected to the highest spiritual values. It was connected to the art of staying alive. It was driven home at every opportunity. I tell you I didn't like it from the get-go, but there did seem to be a ground swell that was unstoppable regarding tasks."

Building a head of steam, Rocko continued his rant, "The one consistently unpleasant task was pooping. Having a bowel movement. As if this were not enough, there was also the auxiliary duty connected to this act. Wiping your butt and then washing your hands. I can remember when they pressed that upon me. 'What next?' I thought.

"The body was our education, and with it, we were to do tasks. We were compelled to act by our very nature. So tasks became a way to measure our life, and we used them efficiently or not for just that purpose. It was all a task. Everything was a task. I mean even procreation was a task. Now with that, I admit that some tasks were more fun than others were, but still it fell unrelenting into the category of a task.

"This bait-and-switch tactic had its culmination in the adult world. There, they brought all this training to bear. There was nothing left of you that was not brought to tasks. They didn't bother to disguise it at all. You were there to carry out tasks. Sometimes they had great purposes attached and sometimes not so great. You now had the tasks at home and the tasks at work. And as if this were not enough, you were encouraged to join some community group who assigned you more tasks."

Red looked a bit perplexed. "Well, what would you do if you were not doing tasks?"

Rocko stopped for a second, hesitated, and said, "No, the more appropriate question is: Is it possible to structure your life without tasks as the super structure? The mind itself has been trained and fitted with a harness for tasks. We are domesticated to do tasks. I'm thinking that maybe this is not all good. Dare I challenge that while still keeping my habit of wiping my bottom?

"Just for a moment let me attempt to explore the possibility of not doing something. Let's examine the elusive idea of lying down our conditioning, of letting go of all the shoulds and gottas. Having consciousness connotates beingness, and beingness can be experienced by just stopping and looking into yourself. This is the unexamined part of us. Distracting ourselves with tasks is sending the Buddha on a fool's errand.

"I suspect we have welded our beingness to doing tasks. It is a welcome splash of relief to think that maybe we could just take a break and rest. Of course we would have to go through a bit of a learning curve to step into nothingness for just a second to see if it's compatible with our life-form. The being part has suffered our ignoring it or only giving it a periodic nod for the last three thousand years. Could we possibly ignore the doing part for just a bit to see what amazing potentials lie undiscovered in the being part of us?"

"You're getting a little crazy here," said Red. "I don't think it really works that way."

"Why not?" asked Rocko.

"Because," said Red, "what we really are is just awareness plowing through reality as it happens to us each day. There is nothing or no one to measure us. It's the canvas of life, and we are the artist."

"Well then," said Rocko, "if you could just be remembered by one task after you're gone, what would that be?"

Red answered immediately, "I like my hens."

It's always hard to tell if a rooster is smiling, but Rocko thought he detected a smile on Red just then.

Rocko smiled. "You've made my argument stronger. How is it that we learn to love, play, dream, produce art, and believe in things we cannot see? In addition, I already know your next question. It's how, isn't it?"

"Well, yes," said Red.

"Don't even bother to ask that question," said Rocko. "You know how. Just go and discover it. That's the fun part. Our being part is ready and waiting for us, like an old suit of clothes. Almost anything in that direction will take you home to it. After all, it is you, and you know it when you breathe, walk, laugh, or see a little child play.

"So for just a bit, lay down your tasks and especially don't measure yourself by them. The whole other part of you is waiting. Well, really be careful though so it doesn't become just another task!"

Rachel the Raven

An interesting character surveys the barnyard every day. Her name is Rachel, and she is a black raven. Well, I guess all ravens are black, but I identify her that way because Rachel has an issue with her blackness. In truth it's not just her blackness that Rachel has an issue with, but the whole raven identity thing. You see, Rachel is quite astute and knows how literature and the media portray ravens.

She always talks about how Edgar Allen Poe described ravens. I mean, in one way, she's quite proud of this portrayal and realizes it brought a degree of notoriety to her species, but on the other hand, she feels like it hinders her own unique exploration of the possibilities of life. Describing Rachel, one could use Poe's quote, "When I was young and filled with folly, I fell in love with melancholy."

This might sound like eccentric behavior for a raven, but Rachel is an interesting character. She always says that she wishes she had limbs when she walks on the ground and celebrates her wings when she flies in the air. The difference and possibilities in those desires not only tease her but give flight to her imagination.

It is just that type of distinction and dilemma that Rachel balances her quixotic existence on. She really is a creature that lives vicariously balanced between reality and the descriptions of the poets. Poe inadvertently describes Rachel again when he says, "I have no words—alas to tell, the loveliness of loving well!"

I don't want to describe Rachel as a total nut ball because she isn't. She's also actually a very practical and reasonable member of the barnyard community. Now even as I say that, it's that very relationship that begs to be explained.

Let me begin by describing this relationship with the barnyard community, and through that, you will see why Rachel stands apart. In most ways Rachel is just a normal raven. She flies in circles above the barnyard, scouting possibilities for food along with her fellow raven comrades. They signal each other with the familiar caw-caw-caw. Now most other creatures don't speak raven too well because the ravens maintain a style of self-segregation, and it's also a very difficult language to learn. This bit of information I received from Rocko the

Mean Butterfly, who says he broke the back of that language only after an intense effort.

He described it as a thousand variations of the familiar caw-caw-caw. While most everyone hears just the same caw sound, the ravens have an intense sensitivity to cadence, tone, and quality that is difficult to describe to non-ravens.

"It is one of the standing jokes in the raven community," says Rocko, "that most other creatures only hear one sound."

He did, however, also admit that it's a very difficult language to keep up with if you don't use it on a regular basis. The other curious thing about ravens is how good they are at gesturing and pointing at things with their beaks.

I only describe this language and other behavior because that's one of the connections that the other animals have with the ravens. Most of them don't like the sound of the ravens cawing overhead. It not that they hate the ravens, but rather the persistent cawing can really get on your nerves after a bit. A good description of this interaction and how the ravens deal with others is what happened with the goats just the other day.

The goats were out in the pasture when a flock of ravens started to circle overhead. Caw-caw-caw went the signal that the goats had stirred up a whole bunch of insects there on the ground, and the ravens were about to take advantage of it. They were closing in to get the insects when the goats got nervous and started to panic at all the movement there above them. Rachel saw the goats were about to bolt and wanted to maintain good relations with the barnyard animals.

Caw-caw-caw came the signal to cease and desist from Rachel. Ravens are nothing if not organized and disciplined. They all grabbed the warm air currents and gained height immediately. Caw-caw-caw came the conversation about what had happened. Caw-caw-caw came the reply from Rachel, who, in a few words, notified her companions that they had panicked the delicate goat consciousness there below.

They have a time-tested alternative when this happens, and with a caw-caw-caw, it was put immediately into effect. The ravens circled widely and landed a good distance away from the goats. They then simply walked over to where the goats were and began to take advantage of all the insects that the goats had stirred up. They knew from many past experiences that the goats would not fear them when they walked in because they were so much smaller than the goats.

In all populations, there is always one who looks around the corner, outside the box, or over the hedge, as it were. In this group, it was Rachel. She assumed a leadership role and guided her compatriots along a finely tuned pose in relations with the other animals. Rachel, you see, believed that anyone not like her had magical powers and communed with a higher power. Now because of this, she was always very respectful of all the other animals. The helping hands have a similar belief in the Hindu population with regard to cows. Similar I say, but not the same.

Now I have to be blatantly honest. Most of the other ravens don't have this heightened sensitivity. Saying this, I have also to admit, within the raven population, there lies murky realms of untold thoughts and dreams. I don't know if this is because of all the illusions, symbols, or hocus-pocus attributed to the ravens or they have, within themselves, cultivated a mystical quality. I'll leave that to those who know more than I do.

What I want to describe here is the effect these curious creatures have upon the larger barnyard community because of this innate sensitivity. Now I know that Rachel leads the charge in a sense because of her particular hypersensitivity, but I also recognize that there is a similar cadence in her followers. Isn't it true that, when you meet someone new, the world is expanded by the unknown experiences of the newcomer? That is what happens with the ravens and the barnyard animals. Is it oily poison or untouched beauty that is conveyed? I'll let you be the judge, but let me just describe a bit more of what is transferred.

I think the best way to describe what the ravens pass into the barnyard community is to quote Poe once more. "You are not wrong, who deem that my days have been a dream all that we see or seem is but a dream within a dream."

The bigger mystery is just how they do that. It proves that there is power, mystery, and magic there in the barnyard community. It also proves that watching others interact usually creates humility. All of that and they still eat bugs and worms.

The Cat in the Barnyard

Last week was the usual normal in the barnyard except for the incident with the cat. I wouldn't even take note of such a small disturbance except for the commotion it caused. I'm somewhat getting ahead of myself here because you first have to understand how this occurred in order to grasp what really happened.

This new animal came quietly and without any fanfare. I only describe it that way because a cat comes with a different energy. Really on another level, it was just a stray cat checking out the barnyard. The first description, however, captures the effect that his arrival had on the other animals in the barnyard. I mean, it's not because there haven't been stray cats in the barn over the years. Several times the cat population has varied in number and kind. This stray was a full-grown tomcat named Skeeter. He knew how to navigate the barnyard even though he was not of it.

Now even though the other animals were very aware of this quality in him, it was not the thing that caused the problem. I might add, however, that it did not help. Skeeter took up residence in the barn in the hayloft. Plenty of mice were there, and Skeeter performed admirably as a mouser. I heard a rumor from some of the other animals who kept contact with the mice population that Skeeter was truly terrifying as a hunter.

It is totally ironic, but the quality that caused the problem with some of the other animals was Skeeter's laziness. It's hard to describe this, but let me just say that Skeeter could relax to the point where it was difficult to believe he had a skeleton. If he were questioned about his relaxation, he simply stated that boredom was king.

Now this in and of itself should have caused no problems. However, the barnyard is a very social place, and when something new arrives and is noticed,;

well inquiring minds want to know. It was just that his ability to relax began to take on notorious accounts. This is something that all cats do, but Skeeter took it to perfection. When he was not out mousing, he relaxed so much that it made you sleepy just looking at him.

Red the Rooster didn't want me to report this, but Denise, one of his hens, initially questioned Skeeter about his boredom theory. It was then probably her social network throughout the area that spread Skeeter's reputation. Anyway, whoever was at fault for the dissemination of this information that eventually grew into a legend is not really the point here. It does, however, describe the thing that occurred. Skeeter became slightly famous for his ability to relax and do nothing.

Still this would not have caused any problems but for another intriguing quirk in Skeeter's personality. He was a stray cat used to living alone and by his wits. This sudden notoriety and elevation of his persona distorted his ego beyond reasonable limits. Skeeter loved the attention and started playing to his new audience. The stage gives veracity to words that have none. It didn't matter to Skeeter. He had the platform, and he was going to enjoy it. The only problem was that his message was a quality just mainly inherent in cats. He began to describe it as if it were for sale and a learned behavior.

Now the animals of the barnyard have a certain wisdom. Saying this does not, however, preclude the fact that they are also very impressionable. In truth, the quality Skeeter was selling was also a forte of the animals in the yard. They also were experts in this ability to be content and let time pass. Finding someone who was better at it than they were was like a carrot on a stick. Never mind that the carrot itself was an illusion. The myth continued to grow.

It really was a strange turn of skills involved in what Skeeter was beginning to sell. If he were not lecturing about his ability to relax, he was relaxing. The whole thing somewhat played into barnyard minds skewed toward boredom. It's a basic fact, however, that each species relaxes and rests in its own way. This essential reality was overlooked as Skeeter the Cat became the measuring stick for yielding to any doing.

Now you ask, dear reader, how this could possibly become a cause for concern in the barnyard? It was the perfect equation: impressionable animals, a silver-tongued cat, and a message that appealed to everyone's nature plus a goal that was impossible to measure. It started a contest among the various animals that was absurd, if not outright funny.

Red the Rooster found that a number of his hens just didn't get off their eggs. Some of the younger pigs didn't get out of their mud bath. Certain of the geese with eyes glazed over were found sleeping in un-geeselike poses. The goats took the prize for doing unpredictable things, however. A number of them were found sleeping on the open ground with all four legs pointed toward the heavens. The other animals had to poke them in order to see if they were still breathing.

It called for an intervention. Red the Rooster was summoned and asked his opinion about how to nip this craziness in the bud. He listened patiently and later contacted Rocko the Mean Butterfly. Rocko actually laughed at the stories and told Red not to worry. He would solve the problem quickly. He gave not a hint of his strategy or plan.

The next day, every time any of the animals started to relax, they saw snakes. It was always when they least expected it and at the most unexpected times. The snakes were everywhere. They showed up just when the various animals were doing common barnyard activities. Now here's the thing. They also couldn't be found when looked for. They appeared at the most in opportune moments but left just as quickly.

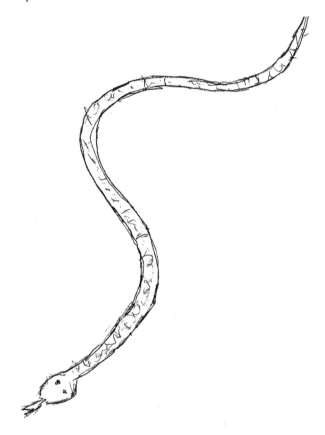

A day filled with catching glimpses of snakes triggered the prey-predator reaction. The goal of relaxation faded quickly from the awareness of the barnyard animals. The snakes stopped coming all the time but returned just as a reminder when the animals started to relax a bit. Gradually things returned to normal in the yard.

Red asked Rocko how he managed the whole thing with the snakes.

Rocko laughed. "That was my friend Rubio and his friends, who are harmless water snakes. He owed me a favor and has always realized the negative image most animals have of snakes. It was fun watching the thing right itself."

Rocko fluttered away, laughing.

The Cow Plop

T his past week I went over to the barnyard to see what was going on. Well, nothing was happening so I walked through the barnyard and headed down into the meadow behind the barn. In the meadow the cows were grazing, along with a number of the goats. The horses have this built-in need to run so they were exercising that capacity down lower in the pasture. Even some geese had brought their goslings into the meadow because the young ones liked the young green shoots of plants that grew there. They stayed up closer to the barn but still ventured out into the meadow periodically.

Why, it was the very picture of pastoral peacefulness. The insects were buzzing, and the flowers were blooming. I took note that the serenity of it all crept into my body like a welcome thief. The sun was not too hot, and a slight breeze caressed your face. I found myself relaxing from the inside out. Happiness is an afterthought when your body finds communion with its environment. I did not want to be anywhere else.

I was enjoying my walk through the meadow, not needing to announce my presence. Everyone there knew who and where everyone was. I felt my foot sink into something soft and gooey. I looked down and saw I had stepped into a cow plop. I looked up and saw that Bossie the Cow, who had probably left this prize for me, was looking at me with total indifference.

This cow plop had stolen my peaceful vision. My sense of dismay came from the incongruity of the previously described and the fact there was cow plop all over my shoe. I just felt in that moment that it was not fair. However, fair or not, I had cow manure on my shoe. Now as I was dealing with this, an old memory came flooding back.

I remember when I was a kid and had my first interaction with cow plops. I had four older brothers, and when we were adolescents, we used to take a shortcut through a cow pasture. I can't remember who started it, but on occasion, we would have cow plop fights. Now you have to realize that we were teenage boys or younger, and boys that age are notorious for finding creative ways to entertain themselves.

The thing we discovered that is probably not generally known is that, when the sun dries a cow plop, it hardens on its underside and top but remains gooey and soft inside. Now to the young mind, this fact led to the realization that you could pick up the cow plop without getting dirty and throw it at your brothers.

"Why?" I hear you saying.

It was the perfect game of one-upmanship. If you were tagged (hit by a cow plop), you knew you had been bested. On the other hand, if you managed to be the winner in this game, there was a solid superiority and success in your step as you walked home.

In addition to that, this torpedo was actually the perfect weapon. It could be carried without coming apart, and once launched, it held together until it made contact with the target (your brother). The impact usually made it break, and the gooey inside part did its work. Now just to be accurate here, there was a degree of sophistication in choosing the right cow plop. If the plop were too dry, it didn't have the desirable inner gooey part, and if too wet, it didn't carry and launch right. There was a lot more to this than met the eye, and it did take a learning curve of practice to choose, carry, and launch a successful cow plop.

In this particular pasture, there were what we used to call pricker bushes everywhere. The cows made paths through these bushes because they liked the scratching as they navigated through these thorny plants. This was the environment where this game of throwing cow plops took place. Now just for a minute, I want to take you along on one of these daring episodes where you had to avoid getting hit by a cow plop, and at the same time, your sole purpose in life was to hit one of your brothers with the aforementioned salvo.

It was a labyrinth of passages, and there were blind spots where you couldn't see where one of your siblings might be waiting with a cow plop. The thing was that being hit by a cow plop was the closest thing to dying we could imagine. The result of losing this contest was you had to walk home smelling very bad while the winner of this contest was mocking and making fun of you. It brought a sense of urgency and intensity to the game that kick the can just didn't have.

I was the youngest in this game so they made a rule that, for me, head shots were ruled out. They only really did that because they knew our mom would be mad if I came home with cow poop in my hair. They were supposedly looking out and taking care of me. I was actually very grateful for this rule because I did have a real fear of getting hit in the face with a cow plop. I can remember the tension of waiting and then the explosive thrill when someone was ambushed. Kids really do make the best games.

I was trying to wipe the cow plop from my shoes that afternoon in the meadow while all this was going through my head. It was a bit embarrassing, but I realized I have a history with cow plops. I looked up toward the barn and saw the geese laughing. They were trying to hide it by flapping their wings and honking, but I know enough about the barnyard to know when I'm being made fun of. It brought back the cruel memory that, more often than not, I did not win at the game of dodging cow plops.

I know it was not logical, but my whole body went through this transformation that I can only describe as humiliation and defeat. It was like I was back in that pasture long ago, being bested in a very serious game of dodging cow plops. It's really true that the mind provides the arena for the acts of our life. I watched, and even though the cow plop was on my foot, it felt as if I was in that long forgotten game with cow plops.

I looked around again and saw that mostly everyone was indifferent. My imagination had given the geese a role they really didn't have. The memory began to fade and, along with it, the tension in my body. I took solace in the few times I had won at the game of cow plop throwing. Sometimes the little things make you happy.

I wiped my foot on the beautiful green grass and went back to enjoying the meadow again. Memories carry things that are both good and bad I guess.

Flies

I was in the barnyard the other day, and not much was going on. I realized at that point that there was an animal with the largest presence there in the barnyard that I've never even mentioned. They are everywhere and keep company with all the other animals. It struck me as funny when I realized that, despite their numbers, I didn't even know if they had a dialect.

The animal I'm speaking of is, of course, the fly. They are everywhere in the barnyard. Their cousins, the horseflies, are especially fond of stalking their namesake and the cows as well. I was curious to know more about these bothersome pests so I went down to the chicken coop to talk to Red the Rooster. He was always very knowledgeable about the relationships among the various animals, both wild and domesticated.

Red was roosting and watching his hens when I came upon him. We exchanged polite greetings, and Red began to go about the chicken business of scratching. I always thought that chicken scratching is the equivalent of our nervous tics.

"What's up?" he asked. "You always have questions for me."

"Oh," I said, "I was just curious if flies have a dialect of their own. In addition I was curious to ask you what opinions the animals in the barnyard have about flies in general."

"The flies don't have a dialect as much as they have a vibration system by which they communicate," said Red. "Also just because they don't have a specific dialect by which they communicate to each other, that doesn't mean they can't understand the other animals. They are one of the most successful species of animals."

This was all very interesting, but it just deepened the mystery I had about flies. "Are they not a terrible nuisance to the other animals?"

"Yes," said Red, "but there is also a relationship established over time gone by that bonds the various animals together. For the chickens and a lot of our other two-legged cousins, the flies are actually a plentiful food source. Some of the larger animals use the flies as a temperature and rain gauge. They know when to stay in their stalls or go out, depending on the behavior of the flies. They are also living company for many of the animals."

In all honesty I found this last example a strange contradiction. "The feeding hands find flies to be obnoxious and dirty to be around."

"Well," said Red, "flies are drawn to warmth, and so are many other animals. And in that seeking, we recognize the life force strong and eternal. In that way, we are all the same. The barnyard animals recognize that flies are insects and live and die by the millions. It's part of the flow of life around us. We understand that this ebb and flow of the life force is necessary for our very survival."

Now this was sort of a different but interesting take on what I thought were just irritating pests. The animals in the barnyard don't worry so much about all the things that we feeding hands do. Reality unfolds in a rather relentless and insistent way for the animals. The advantage they have in that is that the present moment captures them totally. In that, the flies play an ever-present role.

It was really not a very gratifying bunch of information so I went on through the barnyard and down toward the meadow just thinking I'd take a walk and relax. Now I don't know if it was some type of karma or just bad hygiene, but a number of flies began to fly around me. They buzzed me like I was a pile of you-know-what. It was very irritating, and at first I found it a strange coincidence that I was being bothered by the very creatures I had just tried to gather information about.

I swatted them away as best I could, and as we've all experienced, they were relentless and continued to pester me. Eventually as I got down lower in the pasture where the wind was stronger. The flies became less of a problem. I was approaching the stream where there were some flowered bushes and brush, and I was stopped in pleasant surprise as I saw there a hummingbird drawing nectar from some flowers.

Anyone who has come upon this amazing bird that can fly backward is always amazed and entertained. Watching this animal is like being given a gift by nature in time and space. They seem to me to be nature's gifted ability to surprise and delight. Now it was just then because I was again out of the wind and in a space occupied by them that I found myself bothered again by flies.

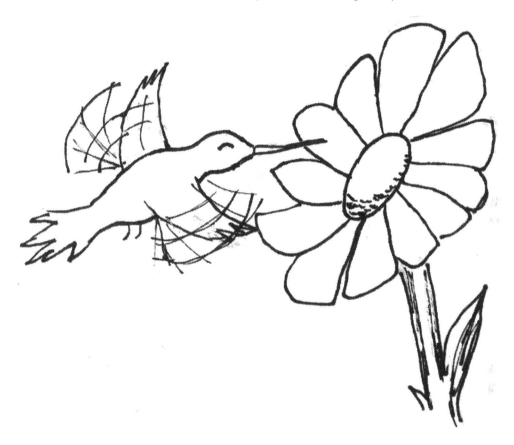

The thought came like a gong hitting a bell. In just that moment, I was struck by the amazing fact that these flies had a lot in common with that hummingbird. Just the fact that they can fly is cause enough for wonder. I know they don't inspire like the hummingbird, but just for a moment there, they did, and it was enough. I saw, just like the hummingbird, they had purpose and ability to pursue it. In that tiny second, I saw one of nature's miracles doing its thing.

I started to laugh even as a number of these annoying beasts was harassing me. If there is purpose, logic, and wonder, even there what an amazing place to plug my curiosity into. I stopped and tried to listen to the vibration of these insects to see if I could discern any logic to their communication. My efforts were not much rewarded. I just heard an annoying buzzing sound that I noted tended to irritate me.

I moved off downstream, trying to outrun my tormentors. They kept pace and continued to do what they do best. In a way it was funny because I knew they could not hurt me. Their job, it seemed, was to just bedevil me. I lost my wonder of them then, which was replaced by the common sense logic that their harassment caused. I swatted at them with my hat and made nasty mouth sounds about their existence.

I returned to the meadow after a bit, where the wind became my ally in keeping these vexing critters away from me. I enjoyed my walk back up to the barnyard and again became reflective about the bounty and diversity of life there in the barnyard. I took notice as I entered the yard that all the animals were going about their business with no distractions or distress.

There, they were again flying around me and buzzing like they had found a prize to torture. My instinct for survival sent a number of these fellows to their eternal reward. I swatted them with gusto and delight. I figured it was just part of a larger plan. Everything was just as it should be in the barnyard.

Family Discussion

Conversations about identity abound. It's the same in the barnyard. One particular conversation caught my attention in the yard. It was about family. Now what constitutes a family? I recognize the deep and fundamental issues involved in a discussion like this, but I was not prepared for the level of intensity that this particular colloquy created. Let me describe what happened and the individuals who participated.

Most times the pigs stay to themselves, but this one young pig named George took to wandering the barnyard, philosophizing about various topics. He wandered over next to the goat pen and was describing one thing or another, and it led to him making the rather categorical statement that we are all family. Well, that didn't sit very well with a number of the goats who were listening to him.

"What do you mean by that? We are goats, and you are a pig."

George was taken back. Not only was he usually totally ignored, no one generally bothered to comment on his long soliloquies. He stuttered a reply that we are all animals.

"Yeah!" countered one of the goats. "But not of the same species."

"Well, actually," responded a goose who happened to be nearby and had been eavesdropping on the conversation. "George has a point. A family can be defined by a group who lives in close quarters and helps one another in tasks of daily living."

A number of goats swiveled their heads in unison toward the goose as she made these comments. As usual there was a lot of talk over as all the goats tried to respond to this comment. Finally Hercules, a billy goat well past his prime, spoke the loudest and made the dogmatic statement that he was not related to any swine.

George was not a sophisticated debater but understood a put-down when one was delivered toward him. His reply turned the tables on the goats when he said, "That's exactly the type of slander used between loving family members."

"Huh!" was almost a group response. The goats verbally stumbled over each other trying to respond.

"Wait," said a swan who had been listening and was now drawn into the debate. "Let's ask Red the Rooster. He's very knowledgeable about things like this."

The goats were a little hesitant to invite Red into the conversation because they secretly knew he was very smart and would know stuff they didn't. Confronted, however, with staring eyes on all sides waiting for their response, they agreed.

"Yes!" said Hercules. "We will consult Red the Rooster in this matter and see what he says."

Everyone knew, however, that Hercules only said that to hold the stage for one more minute when he felt he could be an authority on something.

One of Red's hens who was feeding nearby was sent as a runner to collect Red and have him come to where this very lively debate was taking place. It was not long before Red appeared and asked the gathering how he could be of service to them. The goats all started to talk at once. Red waited while they talked but did not communicate. Finally even the goats caught on to the dissonance they were creating and eventually fell silent.

George the pig spoke, "We were having a philosophical discussion, and I made the comment that we are all family. The goats took exception to this rather broad definition of family. Hercules the Billy Goat said that goats can find each other simply by their smell, and they can't find other animals that way. So the goats have relegated the idea of family to the phenomenon of stink."

This divided the goats into those who agreed and those who understood that George was insulting them. Red listened attentively. A couple of the goats made the point that it came down to a feeling thing. In other words, the feelings created by members of your own group defined the connection to family. George the Young Pig had an agile mind and immediately pointed out that it was also possible to then have feelings for others not necessarily of the same species. Sometimes these feelings were actually more intense and meaningful and led to closer relationships with those other animals.

"Yes," blurted out some of the goats, "but that's friendship and not family feelings."

"Yes," agreed George, "but when those feelings become dependable and deeply meaningful, then those emotions slip gently into the category of what can only be defined as family." Seeing that he had the goats on the defensive, he continued, "It does not necessarily have to be felt as a particular relationship like in a traditional family but rather as a bond to any other who has common interests and feelings."

Red the Rooster was listening to all of this. He could not help but think of his hens in terms of these definitions being tossed about. Next he thought of all the other animals in the barnyard and tried to imagine them as family. In a way, he saw George's point, but in another way, he felt like family was a very special connection that lost power by sharing it too wildly. He also knew in a short time he would be asked his opinion on this matter.

The verbal altercation continued and now seemed reduced to who could yell the loudest. It had attracted a number of other animals from the yard who lined up on either side of the issue. Red noted that he could not predict who would join George or the goats. The pandemonium increased, and logic and reason quietly left the area.

In a moment when everyone seemed to be catching their breath, one of the swans turned to Red and asked, "What say you on this matter?"

In that moment Red became an authority and in the same moment knew he wasn't. Caught a little off guard, he stated, "I will consult with Rocko the Mean Butterfly and give you my answer tomorrow."

There was enough theatre and suspense in that reply that all the animals seemed to accept it. They all would meet back here at the goat pen tomorrow, and Red would have an answer for them. They were all tired out from arguing so they all quite quickly wandered off in various directions.

The next day came. The same group of animals had gathered, waiting to see what Red the Rooster had gathered from Rocko the Mean Butterfly. Red kept the theatrics to a minimum.

He began by saying, "Rocko said that each and every creature fears they are alone in the universe. While that's not true, it is true that, while an individual is in the grip of this fear, it's appropriate to use the idea of family where and when it comforts that individual. We all must belong someplace, and it's just as well to call that place family."

Red turned and left, leaving them all to their very dysfunctional family.

Arthur 51

I was walking through the barnyard the other day, and I passed the area where the goat pen is and noticed something. There is this old goat Arthur who has been around for as long as I can remember. The thing is I noticed something about him that I always knew before, but it struck me as very curious and notable this time around, that, Arthur had no affect or reactions to others around him at all. I always realized this about this old goat, but it never captured my attention before. Now what I'm describing here is rather a curious thing. Most living creatures respond to other living creatures. The social equations necessitates that we take some note of those around us. It's in the genes of all the animals on the planet.

Arthur is the outlier on this. He truly has no apparent reaction to others around him. It made me curious. It made me think of Steven Pearl's famous quote when I looked at Arthur, "I can't believe that, out of one hundred thousand sperm, you were the quickest."

This needed some of my investigative work. I resolved to know more about Arthur. It was really somewhat of a mystery that Arthur could be so out of the social rituals. It seemed to me that, from a distance, he was more of an object than a living being.

I watched Arthur from a distance for a while, and what was confirmed were my initial observations. He was socially akin to a box of rocks. I watched the other animals greet him and go by him, and not once did he initiate a greeting or even a nod of recognition to anyone in his milieu. Arthur was detached, indifferent, and boring. He seemed totally disconnected from the world around him.

Thinking perhaps that he might be deaf, I got one of the geese to go up close to him and honk. It did surprise him and indicated that his hearing was intact. My surveillance produced no other bits of usable information. It was time to go in and meet Arthur and interact with him. Perhaps that would be the most telling and valuable procedure for finding out what made this curious creature tick.

I circled around the barn so I came down through the barnyard like I always did. I wanted to raise no suspicions from Arthur. I think I could have entered with a band playing for all the notice that Arthur took.

I walked over to where Arthur was chewing on some grass. "Hi," I said rather too loudly.

Arthur looked up in my direction, and I saw the eyes of indifference. He did not respond or acknowledge me in any way that I took note of. He immediately returned to the business of ingesting the aforementioned grass.

"How are you doing today?" I asked, trying to get some response from Arthur. It was like the wind across his back. There was no response. "Hey, Arthur," I said rather too loudly. "I want to ask you a question."

He looked up straight into my face, waiting, I guess, for that question. My statement had only been a tactic to get a reply, and I really didn't have a question ready.

"What's your favorite food?" I stumbled. I could see there was a slight flicker of something as the thought was reflected into his eyes. It was nothing I could read, and Arthur went back to his grass.

I stood there next to the goat pen with Arthur feeding on the grass and me struggling with this awkward silence. It did not apparently bother Arthur in the least. I was beginning to think he lived in a different dimension. I started to make conversation with myself, saying things like, "Sure is a great day", and "I wonder where all of Red's hens are."

This brought absolutely no reaction. Arthur did look up now and then between mouthfuls of grass, but all I could see in his eyes was a total blankness and disinterest in his surroundings.

I was very frustrated and stymied. I was actually unable to carry on a conversation with a goat. I admit it was a strange measuring stick, but I had defined the challenge and inserted myself into this. I decided to walk on down and see if Red the Rooster was around. He always had good insights into the animals and barnyard culture. I walked away from the goat pen, and that also got no response from Arthur.

Red was roosting on the fence just below where the chicken coop was. He looked content and happy and greeted me with a warm hello.

"How are you, my fine, tall, two-legged fowl?" he joked?

"Fine," I said. "Listen, I'm trying to start a dialogue with Arthur the goat." Red laughed so loud that he had a hard time catching his breath. In a minute after his laugh, he asked, "And why do you want to talk to Arthur?"

I explained how I was curious about his lack of social skills, and I was wondering if he was really as inept as he appeared. Red cocked his head to the side, looking at me as if I might be the one who was disabled. It made me just a bit uneasy so I continued to explain how I had been watching him, and I was amazed at how dry his response was to the surrounding environment.

"Well," said Red, "you're right about that. Arthur is known for his lack of social graces."

"It's always been that way," said Red. "Well, I remember once when there was a grass fire, and Arthur was downwind. And in the way of the fire, he acted annoyed when asked to move. Everyone has noted his deficiencies regarding social interactions. It's sort of curious because everyone has learned to leave him alone and out of the social current."

"How," I asked Red, "can anyone be quite so unresponsive to those around him?"

Red thought for a moment. "It points to the reality that the opposite of love is not hate but indifference. The only thing we can't afford in our lives is apathy." Red looked sad for a moment. "I feel bad for Arthur, but either the individual has a spark or he doesn't. We are so impressed with our individuality, but the truth is boundaries are the crux of personality. The escape hatch is becoming part of a group. I can't say if this is good or bad but it is what is. We thrive as part of a community. Without the connection to the other, life becomes barren and pointless."

I left after a while once my conversation with Red wound down. He had given me some real food for thought. I walked up through the barnyard and happened to see Arthur still feeding and still alone. A group of kids was playing not far from where Arthur was grazing, and these baby goats were delightful to watch. But they did not even garner any interest from Arthur.

I walked up out of the barnyard, and my mind was whirling with thought. Our minds are sort of a reflection of our community. What we see and the value we place upon things create our feelings. I flashed for a moment on the wasteland in Arthur's mind. I was so glad to have all my friends in the barnyard.

Domestication

T his was a conversation overheard by a goat and then relayed to me so I'm just not sure how much to believe. This conversation supposedly took place last week in the barnyard on Friday afternoon. Rocko the Mean Butterfly had been sitting on some flowers next to the chicken coop when Red the Rooster engaged him in some friendly conversation. Initially the conversation was quite banal and nothing more than a common exchange of polite pleasantries between friends.

Rocko the Mean Butterfly brought up a very interesting question, and Red the Rooster responded so those within earshot began to take note and sort of leaned in to listen to what became a very intriguing conversation or debate.

The question raised by Rocko was, "Which is better: to be free or to be, as they say, domesticated?"

Well, as it was easy to see, there was one of each, as it were, represented here so the conversation not only had tremendous philosophical overtones but sort of a real-life quality to it that captured those within hearing distance.

Red's initial response was that he and his hens were free-range chickens, so he thought he had the best of both worlds.

Rocko responded, "Well, that was like celebrating your imprisonment by describing how big your cell is."

Red, however, turned the tide on Rocko by saying, "There was no way to measure the social contribution of animals in the wild. It is true that the benefits produced by the wild animals are like vague generalities that are not used, measured, or counted by anyone specifically."

Rocko laughed. "The amorphous quality of their charity to the world in general was essentially the very thing that made their contribution so special, valuable, and important."

Rocko maintained, "By the very nature of the terms by which these gifts were spread out into the world, a standard of giving was created. The free animals created behavior standards, relationships, and even baseline values. The essential quality of reality was set by the interactions of these animals one to the other. And all who came after copied the core values set by these initial interactions."

"Well, that might all be true," said Red. "However, isn't this a case of describing the foundation to the larger structure of what we collectively as animals have created. Isn't it true that, until we control our urge to freedom in exchange for collective effort, we really don't accomplish anything of measurable importance? Furthermore, the benefits of domestication to the individual is immense because he doesn't have to fear being preyed upon or suffering the unpredictableness of nature and maybe starving to death in a bad year."

"True," said Rocko, "but by doing that, you're taking the plug out of the bottom of the boat."

"How so?" asked Red.

"The guiding principle to all behavior," said Rocko, "is survival. Once you qualify any individual behavior for the benefit of the group, you weaken the individual. The individual by vast numbers makes the group, and by limiting his individual prerogatives, you also weaken the group."

Red, with his deep and abiding love for his hens, was feeling at this point like a communist or some such other radical. "I understand what you're saying, but isn't it also true that recognizing our position and identity in the group gives us not only power we did not have as individuals but the illusion of an identity that the individual cannot even dream of?"

"Isn't that the seed of the problem?" asked Rocko. "The identity of the animal in the group can be manipulated by a slight breeze or any other animal quicker or a bit more clever than anyone in the group. The only real safe and reasonable path was in being an anarchist."

"Well, how does an anarchist behave?" asked Red.

"He sees real practical problems," said Rocko. "While others are arguing politics, he looks at the reality around himself and makes his own decisions, and he measures everything to his ability to love and contribute to the community."

Shucks, thought Red, *I'm an anarchist!*

"Look," said Red, "I'm a domesticated rooster living in a barnyard with a brood of hens. This whole thing might just be out of my range."

Rocko smiled. "Look, Red, as long as you breathe air, you're political. All politics are local. It's buried deep within your swagger. Don't ever think you can be like your cousin, the ostrich, who puts his head in the dirt and thinks he's not part of the strife. Politics is to us as water is to a fish."

"The cows and pigs seem to get by without engaging this aspect of life," said Red.

"Yeah," said Rocko. "And where do you think hamburgers and bacon come from? To the degree that you ignore the system, you become fodder for it."

Red had to acknowledge the veracity of Rocko's observations and had even heard of situations where chickens were not kept to harvest their eggs but rather to harvest the meat inside their bodies. A cold shiver ran through his noble rooster body at the thought.

"Look," said Red, "I know what you're saying has some merit, but domestication seems to have some aspects to it that are irreversible. I mean, by that, once it becomes established, it cannot be reversed. Why, any one of my hens would be a nice meal for a chicken hawk or a fox if left on her own without the protection of the chicken coop at night."

Rocko thought about that for a second. "I see your point. I think, once a system is established, you have winners and losers within it. Domestication benefits those domesticated until it doesn't. This is the nature of all systems that socialize us. We are their products and victims as well. We cannot escape the treachery of the systems we create. A good example of this is language itself. It benefits us immensely as long as we don't accept the possibility of it defining us."

Rocko and Red seemed to have come to a meeting of the minds, at least on some level.

"Well," they said, "at least we're not in the terrible position of the feeding hands. They seem totally captivated by their creations."

"Yes," said Red, "they wait on us and attend to us like we are the center of their world."

"Yeah," said Rocko, "they appear to be philosophically trapped between freedom and domestication."

If nothing else, Rocko and Red had compassion for the poor feeding hands.

Denise the Farter

Now I received the information for this story from a duck. Everyone knows that ducks are sort of gossips and get into other people's business. I don't think that was the situation in this case, however. It was, it seems, because the story was about a delicate matter in the chicken coop, and both Red and his hens essentially just did not want to air their dirty laundry. That being said, I do not believe I'm violating any barnyard etiquette by reporting these events.

It was a standard day of no noteworthy incidents happening. Days like that in the barnyard were actually very good days. I guess it's because there is a certain harmony in the barnyard when there simply are no occurrences. Everyone goes about their business, and things unfurl just as they are supposed to. It was at the end of just such a day when Red and the hens had returned to the coop and were settling down for the night.

All of a sudden, Red noticed there was a smell in the coop. One of the hens had, as they say, cut one. It was bad. Red's eyes began to water, and he realized this was the kind of smell that you not only smell with your nose but feel in the back of your throat. Now if you've ever been in a chicken coop while the hens are nesting, there is a very pleasant smell to the whole affair. This was a violation of some code that did not need to be written down. The ability to enjoy the coop had been destroyed. Why, the very fabric of chicken society had been torn.

"Hey!" said Red. "Who did that?"

The hens all looked very innocent and confused, except Denise. She looked guilty and embarrassed. Red looked at Denise and could see upon closer examination that she was the culprit.

"My gosh, Denise!" said Red. "Did something crawl up inside you and die?"

This brought a very sheepish grin from Denise. She just said, "It must have been something I ate."

"Ate," said Red. "It's more like an alien has invaded your body."

Denise just sort of sat there and grinned. She didn't know what to say. I don't know if you remember from previous incidents in the barnyard, but Denise is generally known for being a very social chicken. Actually she's been described as a social butterfly. I just give that amount of background because Denise is actually a very likable hen. She actually has friends throughout the barnyard. Now Red was not thinking about all this but was rather suffering this chemical onslaught from his otherwise dizzy, delicate Denise.

It was always part of Red's agenda that he would track down the cause of anything that disturbed the harmony and peace of the coop. This, however, was a difficult situation because it's hard to drain a swamp while the alligators are biting your behind.

Red began his inevitable series of questions. "What did you eat today? Did you eat any of the other animals' meals? Did you overeat. What was your mother's maiden name?"

Now of course, Denise couldn't remember the number of eggs she was sitting on so asking her questions about what she did earlier in the day was a lost cause. Red sort of figured that out about three questions into his interrogations. He decided that what was needed was some stealthy detective work.

The next morning he followed Denise out of the coop and stayed out of sight while he followed her every move. Now the thing was Denise really was very gregarious. Not only did she visit everyone in the barnyard, she had to have a conversation with them all. Red, who was actually a very shy and reclusive rooster, found this all quite disconcerting. However, when he thought of spending another night breathing fowl air, he returned to his detective duties with a vengeance.

Red watched as Denise engaged the geese and carried on a lengthy conversation about the merits of keeping eggs warm before they hatch. Red thought that was like discussing if the sun would come up in the east next morning. She stopped at the goat pen and carried on a lengthy conversation, even though, to Red's observation, no one seemed to even be listening. Next she made the rounds of the stable animals, the cows and horses. They did appear to listen to her but also did not evidently feel the need to respond.

Denise continued to visit all the animals in the barnyard, and Red so far had not seen anything that would indicate or cause an upset chicken stomach. It was, however, coming on toward lunch, and Red had high hopes that this mystery might be solved when Denise got hungry.

Some of the animals started to return to their pens as lunchtime arrived. Red's focus intensified as he wondered what Denise would do at this point in time. She ambled around the barn to where the pigpen was and was greeted warmly by the pigs, who were all just finishing their mud bath. All six of them proceeded to form a procession back to their trough. Denise joined the parade, just like she was one of the pigs.

In front of the trough, all the pigs warmly encouraged Denise to help herself and eat as much as she wanted. The pigs then dove into their meal with a gusto that only pigs can muster when it comes to eating slop. Denise, not one to be outdone, did the same. She started scarfing down that pig food like there was no tomorrow. The only difference between Denise and those pigs was she couldn't make the loud pig noises they made while they ate.

Red's perseverance had paid off. He now understood why Denise had sabotaged her own stomach. His initial instinct was to rush in and stop Denise from eating the pig food, but then he had a thought. Telling Denise to not do something was like spitting into the wind. He thought he might have a better idea.

Later that evening when the hens were settling down for the night, Red waited for the inevitable stink bomb. It came, and Red responded by telling Denise to follow him. He walked across the barnyard and around the barn to where the pigs had their pen.

Red turned to Denise after arriving at the pigpen and told her, "Animals have to sleep with who they eat with. It's a barnyard code."

Denise looked very upset, but hearing this rule, she wanted to be a good barnyard animal so she found a corner of the pigpen and settled in for the night.

The next night Denise returned to the coop, and there were no fowl smells. Things returned to normal, and Denise seemed a bit more aware it seemed to Red. He also noted that he was glad he made up that rule about sleeping with whom you eat with. It had, after all, gotten back his beloved Denise.

It is, however, a good thing to think twice before eating from a trough.

Wizard the Owl

I t's funny when you get so used to some things that you almost don't know that you know it. That's how I felt about Wizard the Owl in the barn. For years, I've seen him there and even acknowledged him at times but have never really given him the time of day. I guess it was because of something Rocko the Mean Butterfly said that drew my attention to Wizard.

Wizard, along with some other owls, have nested in the highest reaches of the barn for years. These owls are interesting because they are amazing birds. Fierce hunters with incredible eyesight, they take second place to no other animal. Now even as I say that, the other quality the owls possess is that they get along with the other animals in the barnyard. They operate on the principle that the best neighbors interact the least and only when necessary.

Rocko and I were having what I can only describe as a philosophical discussion about the necessity of killing to preserve the self. In this conversation, Rocko referenced the owls as a good example of a species that has struck a finely tuned balance in this area. It drew my attention to these otherwise good neighbors. Not that killing to eat put the owls in a category that was subordinate to my way of living. I recognized immediately that, if anything, they might hold the higher ground on this issue because I being an omnivore had others do the killing for me.

The thing that resulted from this conversation that caught my attention was an afterthought by Rocko that Wizard was a very smart creature and was not in the least in any way obvious about that. Now I understand that our world is full of characters that believe they are smart and want to communicate that information to everyone around them. What captured my imagination was that here was somebody who was wise but not scrambling around, bothering to tell anyone. It just seemed like finding the gold nugget in the stream. What could I harvest from this virgin find?

I asked around with all the other animals in the barnyard about Wizard, and their report was pretty consistent. They described a neighbor who was friendly but reserved. Wizard kept to himself and was careful not to encroach upon the turf or territory of any of the other animals. He was polite and even helpful when addressed, but he never inserted himself rudely into anyone else's conversations. Why, it sounded to me like we had an enlightened owl on our hands.

I asked Red the next time I saw him about Wizard's language skills. He told me that owl speak was not all that different from chicken speak, and he had communicated with Wizard on a number of occasions. There was the usual difference between domesticated and wild, but in the owl's case, it did not present a barrier to communication. I was elated to hear this because my skills with chicken speak were quite good, as I had practiced with Red over the years. I could speak to Wizard himself and make my own assessment in this case.

Now the only thing I hadn't figured on was that the owls were essentially nocturnal. They slept the days away and were more active during the night. I made the necessary adjustments to my schedule so I could be available to meet Wizard on his own terms. Now having said that, I really had no idea of what I was getting into. My first interaction with Wizard and some of his fellows was so amazing and different that it astounded me.

I slept during the day and returned after midnight to the barnyard. I walked around to the southern door of the barn, which was left open all night during these summer months. I was walking in to the barn with the intended purpose of finding and greeting the owls. I was just passing through the door when Wizard flew a foot above my head, heading out into the night.

I don't think I can describe the effect that moment had upon me. It was like an instantaneous specter of something out of my ability to imagine. Wizard did not mean to scare me, but his form in full flight with his wings spread wide, moving like a shadow in the night was truly something otherworldly. I experienced what his prey must see just before their lights were turned off for good. It was a look over the fence into another dimension. I felt like a fellow traveler with Dante. I had glimpsed the other side in that moment.

Wizard circled around and landed on the fence just outside the barn. He immediately reassured me that he had not meant to frighten me. I thanked him for his sensitivity and told him that I had come over to the barn to meet and talk to him.

To this information, he was taken aback. I could see I had met a solitary creature, and meeting and greeting was not his strong card. I began to explain my conversations with Red and how he had complimented Wizard and his fellow owls. I was going on into what our dialogue had contained when Wizard, like evaporating water, disappeared.

He was there listening to me, and in the next moment, he was gone. It was almost like he was a spirit. I was left with the silence, and it opened around me all the way to the stars and was totally empty. I had met Wizard.

I walked into the barn, thinking that maybe I'd see some of the other owls. I scanned the rafters of the barn but could see nothing there. Red and some of the other barnyard animals had informed me, if the owls did not want to be seen, they were incredibility good at being discreet. I looked up into the rafters, and there was just a small amount of moonlight. And that didn't play into the barn at all. I felt defeated in my quest but happy I had met Wizard.

I turned and started to leave the barn. I was going through the door when I turned and said in a quiet voice that carried amazingly well in the quiet darkness, "I'd come to the barn tonight to meet Wizard and the other owls. I've heard many good things about them and wanted to meet them and see for myself what I could learn from these wise creatures."

I stopped talking, and in that moment even the insects were quiet. The silence was profound and complete. It seemed to absorb my very body. I waited a second in that total silence and then turned and left the barn.

I returned to the barnyard a couple days later, and Red hailed me as I was wandering about. "I hear you've been making speeches in the middle of the night in an empty barn."

I laughed. "If the barn were empty, how did you hear about it?"

Red chortled. "The owls liked and appreciated your effort at communication. They wanted me to communicate to you that they are solitary and shy creatures and did not mean in any way to offend you. In addition they also wanted me to tell you that their lifestyle of quiet nocturnal aloneness is the creator of their wisdom. If they step away from it, they walk away from themselves. Their ability to see in the darkness also allows them to see into themselves. They said to be patient and, in some lifetime, maybe you'd be incarnated as an owl too."

A Simple Birdsong

I was hanging out in the barnyard the other day, just talking to Rocko the Mean Butterfly. We were not focused on any topic or individual specifically. It was warm, and there was a slight breeze. It's the kind of day that makes you glad you're alive. Red the Rooster came over and joined us, lending us the feeling that just simple companionship feels good.

We were sitting there under the oak tree, and for a while, no one felt like talking. Then the most amazing thing happened. These two songbirds landed on one of the lower branches of the tree we were sitting under. They began a song. It was a birdsong heard a thousand times, I'm sure, by many living creatures. That song told me something that I'll try to tell you.

The two songbirds were Cheep and Chirp, but I don't think that matters, as you will see. I shouldn't prejudice you. Maybe it does. Anyway, let me try to describe what happened. The song that Cheep and Chirp sang pierced my soul. I know some feeding hands say things like that about music, but this was different. I was carried away to a different dimension. I saw that the universe was not out there but inside of me.

This delicate birdsong told me that I was and am a prisoner of my words and culture. It said in the most delicate way that it's up to me to decide what everything in the universe means. I felt the music ricochet inside of me like I was in a big drum, but the sound seduced me like it had delicate wings. It told me my very language was a blunt and crude tool. Feeling the song from the inside, I could reach out and touch its total sadness and joy both at the same time.

I saw that the opposite end of the spectrum from this music was how we treat each other. This simple little song created a wall around me. Inside the wall, the music echoed its lonely beauty. As I listened I was encouraged to look over the wall, and I saw the world dying. There was no good or bad to it. It was just there in all its blatant reality.

A gentle voice inside the music, which oddly was not there, told me that God was a shipwreck on the ocean of time that would not sink. The birdsong, like magic, allowed me to see both sides of things at the same moment. Like a wormhole, I went from universe to universe, and it all happened inside of me. My muscles had no purpose, and my tiny, little simian body surrendered to who I really am. That nothing, of who I am was carried aloft by the birdsong.

No resistance, no preference, no thought, and the music, like light, carried me where even my imagination couldn't go. I felt delighted to finally see what I am. I'm sure it was a glimpse given by unseen forces. The experience had its own power and direction so it could not rest. On it flew like a thousand fables before it. I stopped and looked mostly because I could hardly believe it. They sat there on the branch, two simple birds singing.

I know I'm just muscle and bone and blood and guts, but still the song came and left all that behind. There was no effort to it. I was simply carried away with no will or force to stop it. It was really strange because there was this tremendous energy even while my whole self fell into rest. It was like I was paralyzed by indolence and calmness. I saw that the dignity of the individual depended upon having no external authority.

Along with that came the realization that no one knows anything, and that is as good as it gets. The music gently curled around me and said in no uncertain terms that all ideologies rob your soul. Piled quickly behind and on top of that came the knowledge embedded in the music that, just now, this moment matters. There in that certainty I could not tell the difference between the music and me.

In the moment of seeing, I also saw the underbelly of how we live our lives. I could see that society depended upon repression. It was especially the repression of our sexuality, but it went far beyond that to touch every inch of our lives. The answer followed as if it were connected, and it vibrated through the music like a gift. Look at yourself to free yourself from subjugation to a dying system. Inside the resonance of the music was the unstated idea that it's okay to change your mind, to acknowledge that you've been wrong. The liberation included in that insight almost made me disappear.

I felt myself falling and realized it was into chaos. The part of me still connected to the cultural system panicked. It forced me to say no to a type of behavior that served my past and all the collective history that came before. The moment of decision hit me like a large wave. I saw frozen somewhere the words, "He didn't resist his own extermination"

I saw in an instant that all I had to do was stand up and say no. The music took me there. The realization followed close behind that all I had to do is not participate. It was just a matter of following my own inner voice.

It followed that I saw my life as a scene in a penny arcade. What we strive for in this society has no authentic value. The birds in unison told me that alienation was health in our society. The music went deeper and dissolved some invisible boundaries. I watched from a ledge that the music created, and my ego choked and began to die. The social animal symbolically called the community to rouse the fury of numbers against me. It was too late. The deed was done. I had escaped the herd. The democratic liberation of listening to the birds had freed me.

Doubt measures the level of belief in your life. That's us always trying. Still the music came on. The wind in the oak tree and a million insects all around combined in the birdsong. It was easy to see that the truth doesn't need anyone's belief. It's just there. I could see that our purpose was to look over the edge. Doing that, along with a bit of courage, will take you anywhere you wish to go. Science is ontologically afraid of birds singing and children playing.

It was not just that. The music itself was its own universe inside of me. It told me that the most evil force in our environment is belief. It pushes culture, capitalism, and religions, and these are all games stacked against us. Playing them, we betray ourselves. There is no security in institutions. There was a twittering in the birdsong, and it said that a great change was coming. Encapsulated in the harmony was the knowledge that we as a species are circling the drain.

I saw all this from a quiet, restful place and knew it was up to me to find courage somewhere inside of me. The birds stopped singing and flew away. The oak tree felt like a cathedral. The silence after the music had a painful quality to it.

Rocko turned to me and said, "Now that was a real concert!"

I thought so too.

Quacker

ow I've always taken my job of reporting everything from the barnyard very seriously, but even I have to admit that there is some humor in this most recent experience. It all started about a week ago when I was walking down toward the watering hole. There is this duck in the barnyard they call Quacker. There is a story to how he got that name, but let me first describe Quacker to you.

Quacker is crazy by any definition. The thing is, however, he is actually very pleasantly crazy. He spends his days building castles in the air. I mean, if you are around Quacker, you will notice that his wings are flapping, he is gestulating into the air, and, at the same time, he is quacking away to beat the band. If asked what he is doing, he will respond pointedly that he is constructing a beautiful castle and you should move because the wall that's going up is probably going right where you are standing.

Quacker has a quiet and serious intent to his fantasy-building projects. He appears to attend to the most minute details and spends hours apparently getting it right. Whoever could see these things he is building would surely appreciate the attention to detail and total concern he gives to these creations. The larger problem there is that Quacker is the only one who seems able to see these creations. This fact, however, does not deter him from proceeding with complete and total concentration and enthusiasm. Quacker, by all measurement, is duck crazy.

Quacker got his name because, in duck speak, he has a bit of a lisp. Now to others, duck speak sounds like a series of quacks, but I guess it's somewhat like Chinese in that it's a tonal language. A quack going up at the end means something different than a quack going down at the end of the word. Quacker somewhat gets around this tonal quality of the language by repeating endlessly the thing he is attempting to communicate, and he does this with repetition, pointing, and a considerable amount of pantomime.

The subtle nuance of duck speak is lost on most animals who aren't ducks, but Quacker speaks this language with this lisp, and I guess he makes the sounds with a certain sameness that made the other ducks hear him the way non-duck speakers would. Hence they called him Quacker because he didn't navigate the subtle quality of this dialect. The name along with his behavior was a way of certifying his madness. This also, I might add, had no apparent effect on Quacker.

The intriguing thing about Quacker was that essentially he was accepted with all his eccentricities. The other animals all understood that there was a light on but no one was home. Quacker went about his building projects with a passion that was total and complete, and the other animals either accepted or ignored his behavior. And life went on in the barnyard without a hiccup. Quacker got on quite well, and when he wasn't building something, he was actually quite pleasant and communicated like he was almost normal.

Now Quacker had been going about his business this way for years, I guess, and no one apparently ever saw any reason to try to change his behavior. It actually added a certain flair to the barnyard culture.

Visitors would ask on occasion when they saw Quacker doing something a bit odd, "What's going on there?"

The inevitable answer would be, "Oh, that's just Quacker."

The reason this changed was actually quite intriguing. Apparently Quacker's castles were not only architectural wonders but also inhabited by little, tiny animals that only Quacker could see. What happened was he had built some of his castles next to the run where the barnyard animals went down to the pasture. Evidently some of his tiny phantoms were outside their castle when the cows, goats, and horses were going down to the pasture.

Quacker's apparitions were unfortunately trampled, seriously injuring some and unfortunately killing others. The grief and sadness created by this hallucinatory tragedy was profound. And it had consequences way beyond its illusionary reality. Quacker went into a profound grieving process, part of which involved not allowing anyone to use the run down to the pasture. It was truly amazing the consternation and disruption that one little duck could bring to a community.

The rest of the barnyard watched this imaginary calamity with a bit of baffled bewilderment. They felt terrible for Quacker, but at times, it was a bit difficult to stay focused on exactly why they empathized so badly for him. The other side of the coin was that he was relentless in keeping the barnyard animals off the run down to the pasture. He quacked with his lisp that this was sacred ground. Between his quacking, gesticulating, and plain ol' crying, Quacker became quite a barrier to anyone wanting to cross this haunted scene of ghostly shadows.

Initially the other animals tried to accommodate him, but after a bit, they got tired of going up and around the barn and through the hedge to get to the pasture. It became apparent that someone had to negotiate a new reality with Quacker. I'm not sure if it weren't a bit of guilt on her part, but Mildred the Mare asked Red the Rooster to talk to Quacker and see if they couldn't work something out.

Everyone became quite focused on this impending interaction. It began to take on the quality of two realities crashing into each other. Everyone in the barnyard was very interested to see how Red would resolve this.

Red the Rooster consulted with Rocko the Mean Butterfly.

Rocko laughed and said the solution was actually quite simple. "Quacker is crazy, and that crazy is really a form of simple, and simple creatures like ritual. The solution is to have a funeral for Quacker's illusionary dead animals and move on."

It all sounded immensely reasonable so Red set about the task of arranging for the barnyard animals to have a funeral for the dead and unseen creatures of Quacker's castles. A number of matchboxes were obtained and placed on the wagon pulled by Mildred the Mare. Quacker was instructed to place his dead castle tenants into these makeshift caskets. He was then informed that the whole community would attend to their eulogy and burial as befitted these important avatars. A long line of animals stood in respectful silence as they waited to begin the procession down to the pasture where Red had made ready a burial site with appropriate markers.

The whole thing came off quite nicely. Some of the eulogies presented were a bit vague because no one really had any personal knowledge of these pretended individuals. However, Quacker seemed somewhat comforted by all the attention to his lost friends. After the funeral, like all good funerals, there was extra feed all round.

Things returned to normal in the barnyard in the following days, and everyone was careful not to infringe even close to Quacker's castles.

Printed in the United States
By Bookmasters